Gamebuster

Gamebuster

Annabel and Edgar Johnson

COBBLEHILL BOOKS

DUTTON   NEW YORK

Library of Congress Cataloging-in-Publication Data
Johnson, Annabel, date   Gamebuster.
Summary: Overhearing what seems to be a bomb plot and discovering
a dead body in the trunk of his car are only the beginnings of a
dangerous adventure in which a high school senior rediscovers his
father, an undercover agent, and becomes involved in a fight against
dispossessing the Navajos of their lands forever.
[1. Fathers and sons—Fiction. 2. Mystery and detective stories. 3.
Navajo Indians—Fiction. 4. Indians of North America—Fiction] I.
Johnson, Edgar, date. II. Title. III. Title: Game buster.
PZ7.J63015Gam   1990   [Fic]   90-1330
ISBN 0-525-65033-4

Published in the United States by Cobblehill Books,
an affiliate of Dutton Children's Books, a division
of Penguin Books USA Inc.
Published simultaneously in Canada by
Fitzhenry & Whiteside Limited, Toronto
Designed by Mina Greenstein
Printed in the U.S.A.
First Edition   10 9 8 7 6 5 4 3 2 1

TO HOLLIS

Gamebuster

Pre-Game Show

❑

THE NIGHT was dense as black water, a million light-years deep, drowning the stars to thin points. It overwhelmed the high peaks of Colorado's Rockies and lay heavy on the heights of the vast Uncompahgre Plateau, flowing down around the cluster of houses isolated in one of the valleys. As the yellow window patches winked out, darkness closed in on the town, settling in a pool at the bottom of a deserted stadium.

In the inky silence echoes vibrated . . . *And now, ladies and gentlemen, the Twin Forks Lightning is coming out onto the field. At quarterback, the one and only Scott "Drummer" Drummond!* . . . as a long-gone crowd tore the air to slivers.

Halfway up the empty grandstand a shadowy figure hunched motionless except for an occasional shudder. Too cold for mid-November. The frigid rawness of the air corroded its way inside his field jacket. A light jacket, it was meant for crisp autumn afternoons, a few minutes on the bench. Not to bog down here at midnight, watching a ghost-game.

Below, on the invisible gridiron, players lined up—crashed together in fierce combat. One stepped back to elude the rush. *He's out of the pocket, scrambling, the ball spirals—it's on the money! Touchdown!*

But the memory was from another life. Ten days ago. The game with Delta—Scott could barely recall being carried off the field, special effects blasting around his brain. In a swaying shuttlecraft with white-coated aliens hovering, he had tried to struggle. No use, tied hand and foot. Only when the fog cleared, later in the hospital room, he realized his arms and legs were totally disconnected. Things got real in a hurry.

It took two hours of pins and needles before his body began to work again and he could drop a few inner words of sincere gratitude to Somebody, whoever. Then they told him the rest of the story. The doctor was hiding behind a lot of medical mumbo jumbo, but eventually he had to get to the bottom line: "Scott, take up a nice safe sport like skydiving. Or skiing, or ice hockey, or climb Mount Everest—anything where you don't use your head as a battering ram. Otherwise . . ."

Meanwhile, poor Mom is trying not to turn pale. And Clint, good old Clint, like a chunk of granite, half-paralyzed himself. "You're going to be okay, son. That's the main thing. Don't sweat the future right now." Clint, who loved the sport like a fool. Clint, who never had a son of his own, but had given a kid his name and his trust and a red Mustang with only 30,000 miles on it last year after Twin Forks took the Triple A title. "You've got plenty of time to think what comes next." Sure, do anything you want—except play the game. Ever again.

That was the toughest thing, to conceive of a life without football. No Big Ten scholarship, no Heisman, no Number One draft pick, which everybody said you were a cinch for. And of course no million-dollar contracts, no Super Bowl. No more dreams.

In the dark of the stadium, Scott couldn't even shiver anymore. The core of ice in his gut was spreading, turning him brittle. He felt—colorless. It had begun back in the hospital; that place would drain the red from a radish. Even your visitors begin to fade after a couple of minutes. Girls, their hair wilts and their feet keep wandering toward the nearest exit. You aren't the poor wounded hero this time; you're yesterday's news. The guys on the team can't help hating you for getting messed up just when Montrose is coming in on Saturday and we need the game to make the play-offs. Then they feel guilty for being mad, and they kid you half to death, but they leave fast. Even Coach was trailing shreds of hurt behind the sickly grin. "Take it easy, Drummer."

Take it easy? If one more person said that—

The only one who hadn't was old Gilly. Trust Miss McGill to brighten your day with an English assignment, right there among the oxygen equipment and the IV tubes. "It's a chance for you to bring your grades up, Scott. I'll accept a report on this article for makeup credit." Then when she was gone he'd realized it was her peculiar contribution to his get-well fund. The piece was titled "Olympics of the Mind." So she wanted him to remember he had a brain, great. But if you want to know, he informed the empty air, eggheads don't get their faces on the old Wheaties box.

Not that he wanted to be famous. Or even rich. Well, maybe that was part of it, but the main reason he'd invested himself so totally in the game was simple: It feels so completely great to be good at a thing, really good. To lead the other guys, to feel them counting on you. Pick the play that will win, or read the defense and call a different one.

Next time I yell a signal it will probably be "Big Mac with catsup, hold the onion."

The ice in his middle cracked sharply; he could feel its sharp edges raking his ribs. To hell with the doctors. Why not go back onto the field, take your hits, and if one goes wrong, so—there are worse ways to end it than under an afternoon sun in a stadium going bug-guts.

Except it wasn't that simple. The neurologist painted a different still life: After all the tests, what it came to was one more head-on collision and a certain defective vertebra in your neck might telescope into the next like a folding cup, ruining your spinal column—you're a rutabaga. For the next sixty long years of bedpans. Are you really ready for that?

The planks of the bleachers were cutting into his rump, which was so numb it hardly noticed. *Maybe I'll get lucky and freeze completely to death; they say it's a peaceful way to go.* Tomorrow they'd find an ice sculpture, hang a name-plate on its backside: End of a hero.

Then the wry thought took an odd bounce. Why not? No anticlimaxes. No petering out for years in some dull job, no bosses or income tax. No arthritis; you'd never grow old. Leave the stage while you're still "the Drummer." There'd be a dignity in it; you'd be in control just as you've always been on the field. Run the old "Game-buster"—Coach's code name for the big play where you call your own number, carry the ball yourself, across the middle, over the goal line, end of game.

He seized on the thought so fast he made himself draw

back. This kind of decision you can't change your mind later, so consider all the angles. Like, how would you do it? Not really freeze—stiff is ugly. You'd hate to wind up with your picture in the paper looking like a side of meat. Nothing bloody, either. And hanging is for horse thieves. But there must be some neat way that wouldn't gross people out. Faceless in the night, Scott began to hone the edge of this dagger of the mind. . . .

From somewhere came an intrusion on the stillness, a nagging mutter that irritated, then puzzled him. Voices seemed to rise from below the stands. Eleven-thirty, nearly midnight, who'd be spooking around? Out of the mumble a word or two began to surface.

". . . it iss a matter of timing . . . must be in place by middle of December . . ."

". . . don't understand my problem. These people . . . no concept of a deadline."

"*Dead* line? Your languich iss most colorful." Some kind of oily accent. ". . . may help raise their ent'usiasm when the rest of pretty toys arrive at the Shay next veek."

"Maybe not. These people aren't exactly into bombs. Even if we can recruit them, they'll need some instruction. And time will be a factor if we're to coordinate with cells, in London and Paris and Rome. Communication at the camp is pretty primitive, too."

They were directly below him now. Scott could hear the words distinctly as the foreigner said, "Primitive you don't know. Primitive iss Pakistan. Primitive iss jungles of South America. Some parts of the vorld the natives don't even know iss soon to be the new century. Do not concern yourself—the Shah-man has his finger on the detonator. In six weeks, the year two t'ousand will dawn like thunder."

"More like the Fourth of July," the other sniggered. "The

[5]

loudest New Year's Eve show the world has ever seen. All those 'Century' parties they've got planned in every big city—like they say, it'll be a blast. Of course, some will be easier than others. The roof of the Astrodome will come down like Armageddon. The Omni, too. But outdoor arenas like the L.A. Colosseum will need extra personnel to set the charges. And the downtown crowds in places like Times Square will be tricky."

"Which iss why ve need your Operation Monster Slayer, my friend . . ." They had moved past now, their voices fading into the black regions below.

Hardly able to believe what he'd just heard, Scott ran the conversation again, the way he memorized a new set of plays. Finally, uncranking his numb legs, he got up and moved in the same direction, cautiously. It occurred to him that if, by some far-out chance, those yoyos were on the level, they wouldn't appreciate an eavesdropper. But when he reached the exit there was no sign of them, no movement in the parking lot.

As he got into the Mustang he wondered if they had seen it. Of course there was no way they could connect it to him. And it was none of his business anyhow. Except, if they really were planning some kind of sabotage for New Year's Eve, stadiums wall-to-wall with families, little kids—"Please, mama, let me stay up and see the fireworks!"—it better be somebody's business.

Slowly he drove home through the sleeping town and the darkness, which was not just all around him now. It had wormed its way inside and found a brooding place.

SCOTT

□

MORNING SHRINKS the world back to normal, but it doesn't shed a whole lot of light. Not on one of those overcast days in November where the sun is only a cheap imitation up there behind a sheet of wax paper. That high wintry haze meant weather. Scott just hoped it would hold off until after tomorrow's game.

Marhofsky's fingers are going to be sweaty enough. Rain or not, concentrate on the running plays. Silently Scott beamed advice at the team, who were over in the gym right now for the usual Friday strategy session. Coach had invited him to sit in, hang around the bench tomorrow and help send signals. Don't they realize that when I'm there, Marhofsky turns to all-thumbs? Give the guy a break. Let him be the star for once; maybe he'll come through for you. Just keep the play on the ground so he can hand off fast. Montrose is a sack-pack, and he couldn't scramble his way out of a grove of dead hollyhocks.

The tall weeds stood, brittle and brown, all over the

[7]

vacant lot. Scott scooped the top off one—a shriveled dead blossom. Moving slowly, he scuffed through a patch of cockleburs. Wouldn't want to be early for the appointment. Actually he hated the whole idea. But what else can you do?

Ever since last night, that business over at the stadium kept feeling weirder. It didn't make any sense—voices in the dark. He knew it was going to sound hokey. And yet he had to spill it to somebody. Maybe if Clint had been home—"Hey, want to hear something crazy?" But Clint was in Oklahoma, big emergency on one of his oil rigs. And you don't mention it to Mom—she'd run to the sheriff, who would snicker all over his cop car. He and the clowns down at the police station would have a ball. "Old Drummer really wigged out—poor kid, y'know what he's been doing? He goes over to the stadium at midnight, just sits there. He thinks he *hears* things." Or maybe they'd figure it was a play for attention, now that he'd lost the spotlight. Uh-uh, cops were out.

Of course there was one phone number he could call. It had been at the back of Scott's mind from the beginning, but every time he thought about it he thought *no*. Not a chance. No way.

Better the FBI. At least it's anonymous. The guy he'd talked to on the phone obviously never heard of "the Drummer." Which was fine. You pass the thing along to the feds and you've done your duty. Let's get it over with.

He crossed the loading zone behind Safeway, went around the store and out onto Mesa Street. The clock on the courthouse showed seven minutes to ten. Picking up the pace, he headed for the old pile of granite.

Back stairs smelled as if a thousand drunks had been hauled up to the holding cells on the top floor. Down a corridor he passed a lot of closed doors until he came to 311. The outer office was empty, steno's desk clean and the typewriter hooded. No flag. No picture of the President on the wall. Small, it didn't look like a Regional Office of anything. It sure didn't look like the FBI.

The man who opened the inner door did. A Brylcreem type with steel-edged eyes and a mouth like a coin slot. He had shaved so close he'd nicked himself—the Band-Aid under his chin couldn't be covering a zitz. No pimple would dare touch that jaw. From the breast pocket of the three-piece suit a sly wedge of white handkerchief showed. The shoes were real leather, the tie was raw silk, and he was Norman Holdrege. The sign on his desk said so.

"Drummond, right?" He waved a hand, sit down. "You phoned earlier, said you wanted to report some subversive talk you overheard?" Settling behind a gray steel desk, he got out a yellow tablet and wrote across the top: DRUMMOND INTERVIEW, and the date.

Scott didn't feel like the stiff-backed chair; he roamed over to the window. Great view of Penney's parking lot. But what he was really thinking was, how do you get across the creepy feel of those words crawling up at you in the midnight darknesss? "I know this will sound weird," he began, "but, see, I happened to be over at the stadium last night . . ." He gave it his best shot, while the FBI doodled. A picture of a bird—Holdrege gave it a fantail like a turkey.

"Sounds to me like a couple of nuts planning a party," he said at last. "Lot of these fools like to set off cherry bombs on New Year's Eve. Especially this year."

"They used the word 'detonator.' You don't detonate firecrackers. They were talking about explosives, and bringing down the big arenas and killing a lot of innocent people." Scott tried to keep his voice even, but this guy's aftershave was beginning to make him sick. "Why would they meet under the bleachers in a stadium to plan a party? At midnight?"

"For that matter, why were you there?" Holdrege stared at him like a trout under ten feet of cold water. Then he could see Scott's face getting red; he lightened up. "Look, I'm not saying you hallucinated the whole thing—maybe you did hear—who knows what? But you didn't see these characters' faces, you couldn't identify them? So what do you want the Bureau to do?"

"Hell, I don't know. Alert the airports. Check out the town for strangers. Hunt for clues under the stands or stake out the place in case they come back. You tell me—you're the FBI. Isn't that your job, making the world safe from the bad guys?"

"Not really. We specialize in the USA." Holdrege doodled a flag waving over the turkey. "For saving the world, contact the CIA."

"Okay, so give me a phone number to call."

The G-man almost laughed. "Can't do that, I'm afraid."

"You telling me you don't know their hotline?"

"I'm telling you I can't give it out."

"You mean you won't." Scott could hear himself about to boil over. "Because you think I'm some kind of freak." *Get out. Now.* He headed for the door.

The G-man strolled after him. "Let's just say I think you've been watching too many James Bond flicks on the late show. Listen, friend, we appreciate your public spirit—"

Fizzle, sizzle, pop! "I didn't come here on a civics assignment! I came to head off some bombs. If you don't want to believe it, fine. Only when you go out on the town next New Year's Eve, don't be surprised if you come down with a sudden case of dead!" By now he was through the outer door.

Along the hallway people were glancing out of offices to see what the yelling was about. Scott could feel their frowns following him as he booted down the stairs. Out along the sidewalk like a track meet—he made himself slow down. Don't get mad, get even. One of his main rules of combat, it had taken the team across a lot of goal lines. Make the stupid jerk eat dirt. Only how? Write a letter? But it wouldn't get to the right department for weeks, and there isn't that much time. The Fiesta Club has already hung out its sign:

Make Your Reservations
A NEW CENTURY ONLY COMES ONCE IN A LIFETIME
CELEBRATE WITH US!
Dine, Dance — Formal Attire

Lousy monkey suit—I wouldn't even want to be buried in one. The words caught him up short, turning an idle thought into a shaft. No sad Sunday clothes. You'd want to go out wearing the uniform, of course. Plenty of color—bright turquoise with the silver zigzags down the shoulders to symbolize lightning, and the helmet with the stars. The coach had started the star thing last year, pasting on a new one for each TD pass. How many now? No big deal, but the crowd liked it. Clint loved it. He'd make sure the funeral instructions were carried out.

Are you off your reel? You don't end it all just because a few plans got changed (completely wiped out, gone, zilch, a professional career down the drain). You brace up and enroll in some business school, get your MBA (and sit behind a lousy desk while your muscles rot). Or learn the ropes of the oil racket, like Clint once suggested (while the guys on the rigs call you "daddy's darling" behind your back).

Scott found himself standing in front of Walgreen's. *Why did I stop here?* Oh, yeah, the pay phone. By some miracle it still had a directory attached. Just curious, he thumbed down the government listings and found the CIA. Denver exchange, probably get some secretary who never heard of Twin Forks, Colorado. Picture what she'll think when an unknown voice calls up from the west slope with a wild story about terrorists.

Of course there are unlisted lines at Langley where you don't go through a switchboard, you get a live agent on the other end. Shoving his hands in the pockets of the field jacket, Scott walked slowly on, thinking.

Thinking of that one phone number, exactly as he'd sworn not to.

MAYBE HE should wait and discuss it with Mom. But she wouldn't be home until late afternoon; Friday was her volunteer day for Meals on Wheels. And he'd rather keep her out of it anyway.

When he let himself into the big house, the quiet was furry with the hum of the fridge, breathing of the furnace, all the things you hear when it's empty. Upstairs, the drip of the faucet in the bathroom seemed loud. An antique clock ticked away the minutes on the wall of the master bedroom. Scott hesitated at the door—he hated people invading his own room. Then he went through quickly, embarrassed by the Aqua Velva snuggling up to the Oil of Olay on the dresser.

Beyond, the sun porch felt more neutral. A bright place

with windows on three sides, brushed by the bare branches of the locust trees. You always felt like a bird up here, looking across the top of Twin Forks, off to where the ragged rim of the Uncompahgre was starting to get socked in by low gray clouds.

When Scott sat down at the little rosewood desk, he could almost feel his mother's vibes. It was right here a couple of years ago, she'd shown him a letter. "I've just heard from Jonah," she said. "He's sent me a number—it's a private line." On a square of plain blue notepaper were a string of long-distance digits that looked like the national debt. "In case you ever have an emergency when Clint and I aren't around—if something happened to us and you needed help—you can reach him here."

He hated to admit he had this curiosity, but it bugs you—the idea that your blood comes from some total stranger. My *father*. The word was just a technicality, he couldn't make it seem real. "So what else did he say?"

"Not much. Just that he's left the CIA and is free-lancing, whatever that means." She always sounded sad and a little angry when she talked about the man she was once married to.

"I don't get it. Why doesn't he ever call us up? Wouldn't he like to know how we are?" Wouldn't he like to speak to his own son just once, for crying out loud?

His mother gave that small shrug. "He feels the less he has to do with us, the safer we'll be. His work for the Company was very dangerous. And now that he's off doing some sort of undercover thing on his own, I suppose it's worse. He told me once, the only time he feels alive is when he's risking his neck to wipe out some sort of—I don't know—evil. It's what Jonah thrives on." She was tearing the letter into small pieces. "I'm just as glad he keeps his contacts with us to a minimum." She threw the scraps away and put the paper with the phone number in the back of her address book. Then reaching out, she gave him a pat on the cheek, the way you touch your prize possession. "Your father would be very proud of you, I know. But try to put him out of your mind."

Scott sat staring at the blue paper with the writing that looked foreign—a hatch through the seven—trying to get some sort of feel of the guy. But he was drawing blanks. Roughly he began to punch the buttons on the white extension phone. By now the line had probably been disconnected.

It was ringing.

After a minute there came a series of noises, clicks, as if a computer were transferring it. Another short silence and another click. A low voice said, "Yes?"

"I'd like to speak to"—the name stuck in his throat, he'd never said it aloud before—"to Jonah Pike."

A pause. "Who wants him?"

"My name is Scott Drummond." Drummond, for the guy who raised me all these years.

"Go on."

"Are you—?"

"That's right. Is there a problem?" The tones were so level it was hard to picture the person on the other end.

"I wondered—I thought you might be able to tell me— I know you're not with the CIA anymore, but maybe you could give me a number there to call where I could report a bomb plot."

After a second the voice said, "Have you talked to your local police?"

"Our cops aren't exactly—this is way over their heads. And the FBI couldn't care less. They said it was too international for them, because— Well, I heard these guys mention setting off bombs in Rome and Paris and London, and they mentioned the Shah of Iran—"

"Iran doesn't have a Shah anymore."

"Oh. I thought that's who they meant, they called him the 'Shah-man.' "

Dead silence for the space of a long breath. Then, "Start at the beginning. Where did you hear all this and when?"

"Late last night. I was hanging out at the football stadium alone—" *And if you ask me why, I will hang up so fast your ear will look like a dried fig.* But there were no interruptions. The silence listened as he recited the story. He could feel the information being ground up and chewed. Finally, he added, "Maybe it's a lot of hogwash but I figured I ought to do something."

"Do nothing," said the voice with slight emphasis. "Not anything at all. Don't even follow any leads if they fall in your lap. Don't discuss it with anybody. Sit tight. Act normal. And don't go roaming around that stadium again at night. In fact, stay home after dark. Leave the investigating to me." Dial tone.

Scott put the phone down and sat looking at it. *And by the way, son, how are you these days?* The man's human warmth was overwhelming. No wonder Mom got the divorce. Scott was thankful he'd left her completely out of this, as he put the slip of paper back in her address book.

At least he was rid of that problem. Now he could let himself consider certain other matters, but not here. Hurrying past his own room—he hadn't had time yet to yank the stupid trophies and pennants—he bolted downstairs and out the front door into the listless light of noon. Over on the western edge of that plastic sky, a grayness was thickening, but maybe it wouldn't arrive until after the game tomorrow. Not that it really mattered. Or ever would again.

SCOTT

[ii]

◻

IT WAS a whole new ball game—no figure of speech. The lineup on the field looked like a schematic diagram, when seen from high in the stands. Scott slouched low in the shapeless bulk of an old Mackinaw, ski cap down around his ears, heavy snowshades putting up a blank front in case anyone noticed him.

Which they hadn't. It wouldn't occur to them he'd stick around as a mourner at his own wake. The scene in the locker room had been bad enough. When he'd dropped by awhile ago to wish them luck, nobody said it. Nobody said, "You look okay to me." Or, "Couldn't you have toughed it out till the end of the season?" After all, they didn't want to speak ill of the chicken-hearted. Coach even clapped him on the back. "No big deal, Drummer. It's just a game, right?"

Wrong. That, going on down on the fifty-yard line—the competition, the demands you put on yourself to hurl your body in the air higher than you could possibly leap, to throw the ball farther than you ever did before, to control the play with an effort that's practically superhuman, to see it work, to win, with the crowd screaming their throats to cheese graters—that is the hot coals of life. Without it, you're a cinder block.

And so is the team. The poor damned linemen were trying to protect Marhofsky, but they weren't used to a QB who has to stay in the pocket. By the fourth quarter he'd been sacked so many times he must feel like potatoes. For a few minutes it looked as if they might get lucky. A Montrose back missed an assignment and Kessler jinked through the hole, down to the 8-yard line. First-and-goal. Scott was on his feet, choking on unyelled advice.

"Option—run the option!" The girl at the far end of the bench supplied the vocal. The only other person who preferred the altitude of the back row, she was jumping up and down, slapping her pink mittens together. Groaning as Marhofsky got decked again back on the eleven. "You're going the wrong way, dummy!"

Second down, the poor guy dropped the snap. He managed to fall on it, but the third was an incomplete pass. When the field-goal unit came on, Scott didn't want to watch. Ulrich could barely kick his bedroom slippers across the room. So follow the play through the girl's reactions: Her fuzzy mitts take the snap, her knee twitches as the kick comes through. Shoulders plead with the ball, left, left, left. And then she leaps straight in the air, pixie face split in a happy yell. "Yeaaaaa, Twin Forks!" From under her pink stocking cap, brown curls burst into applause.

Of course it didn't last. When the game was over, Montrose walked off with a 17-3 win. As the crowd funneled toward the exit ramp, Scott was right behind the girl. He wondered why he'd never seen her before. Actually, it was a relief to be utterly unknown to somebody. Maybe, he thought, he could ask her out for some hot chocolate at the doughnut joint and they'd talk about the game like two ordinary people. At the exit, the crowd shoved them together and she gave him a smile. Slightly crooked teeth made it a little quirky.

"Tough loss," she said.

"Yeah."

"Things haven't changed a bit. When I was in school here, Montrose beat us four years straight. But I'd heard the team got better lately." Not exactly pretty, she was sharp-looking. And older than he'd thought, probably college.

"You live in town?"

"I used to," she said. "Now I'm just on my way through. Stopped to see my mother. I've got a new job, my first big one." The vivid blue eyes brightened with anticipation. "I've been accepted on a dig down in Arizona. I'm an archaeologist."

Scott wished her well, but right then he couldn't bear to sit around and listen to a lot of talk about wonderful futures. It made him feel tongue-tied, mind-tied, which had never happened before—not with a girl. They were out in the parking lot now and she was waiting. All he could say was, "Well, lots of luck. See you around." It came out flat and abrupt. Her smile went away. *Sorry about that, but it's a long story.* He flipped his hand and headed for the Mustang.

Across the lot a couple of kids were getting in their car. "Hey, Drummer, you shoulda been in there, you'd-a clobbered 'em."

Scott kept going. Who the hell is "Drummer"?

* * *

GEORGE BUFORD could have been wondering the same thing, the way he kept glancing across the table. Scott could feel the man trying to put a finger on what's-wrong-with-this-picture? Nice house, good dinner—Mom is always a great hostess. She had probably asked the guy over on purpose so we could all pretend things are normal. Might be easier around a stranger. Or more likely, it was a case of kindness. She felt a sort of pity for out-of-town fund raisers.

This one was typical—bald head, suit by Sears Roebuck, and sad bifocals that kept straying back to Scott like a lost dog.

"Mr. Buford is with NAV," she was saying. "That stands for Navajo Assistance Volunteers. He wants me to found a chapter here in Twin Forks." Helene Drummond, known to be the softest touch in town, Scott thought fondly. A complete lady from her neat jade earrings right on down to her tiny green pumps, coordinated with the green wool suit. He wondered what the Indians would think of her. Probably make her an honorary princess. He had never known anyone more royally put together. Until these last couple of weeks. For a while she'd almost come apart. He could still see the cracks when she looked at him with those worried eyes.

So you're going to make it worse? Make it permanent? Hurt her some more? Not really. If I was gone, she'd cry for a while and then she'd begin to heal. A lot faster than if I'm stumbling around the house, learning to be mediocre. There are worse things than—

"—death," Buford was saying. "It will be the end of a whole beautiful culture."

Scott struggled to get back into the flow. "You mean the Indians? Somebody wants to *kill* them?"

[20]

"I'm afraid it may come to bloodshed," the man said gravely. "The Navajos won't be forced off their reservation again without a fight. They were displaced once before, back in the 1800s, and it was almost the end of the Nation. They are so deeply tied to their native land, when they're taken from it they lose their spirit, their sense of who they are."

Scott could buy that. "But who's gunning for them? Why?"

"It's the minerals, dear," his mother explained. "The Corps of Engineers has discovered valuable deposits down there. They want to strip-mine large areas and set up milling operations."

"You see, we're in a war," Buford added soberly. "An economic fight-to-the-death with Japan and China and Korea. And right now we're losing it. While we weren't looking, back in the '80s and '90s, the Third World countries of South America and Africa began to grow up. They nationalized all their raw materials, which we once tapped at will—manganese, chrome, bauxite, tin, and so on. They've made trade agreements with the Eastern bloc, which now has a virtual monopoly on many minerals that are vital to industry. It gives Japan and Korea a big edge over us. Some of our leaders feel that a few Indians can't be allowed to stand in the way of our country's economic survival. They've introduced a bill in Congress that would dispossess the Navajo forever. Of course others of us think it's not ethical to break the old treaties. We're trying to raise funds to fight the bill, at least delay it until we can come up with a compromise. But the backers of the legislation are pushing to bring it to an up-or-down vote right after the first of the year."

Scott was only halfway listening. He was very aware of

his mother watching—she measures me in food. Why can't I gag down a few more potatoes?

"Excuse me while I get dessert," she was saying. "I made a hot apple cobbler."

Just his favorite, of course.

Meanwhile Buford was studying him openly now, as if next Friday there will be a quiz. "Forgive me, but I can't see much resemblance between you and your mother. You're a husky blond and she's so small and dark. You must take after your dad."

How would I know? I never saw a picture of him. Mom says he wouldn't let a camera within a mile.

"Sorry I missed him," Buford went on. "When is he due home?"

"Clint? I don't know, sir." Scott was on his feet. "Excuse me if I eat and run, but I've got to go over and collect the gear from my locker. Good luck with the fund drive."

His mother had just come back, carrying dishes that gave off a steam of cinnamon and nutmeg. Trying to blank out her look of dismay, he made an end run for the front door. Out in the driveway Buford's rental car squatted, pudgy yellow Toyota—kind of suited the guy. Scott skirted it to get to the Mustang, the only place he felt halfway normal anymore. He was thankful it smelled of old pizza and flat Pepsi.

The clouds were on the move now, coming in low, smothering the last of twilight. As he drove, the windshield was suddenly covered by a fine fur of mist. Scott flicked on the wipers—only a few blocks and the car turned in automatically at the stadium parking lot. When he got out, the wind slapped him in the face like a wet towel.

Using his own key, he let himself into the building—one

of the perks of being a star, except this time he felt like a trespasser. In the locker room his hand found the light switch. The blaze of brightness made him nervous. There weren't any windows, but suppose one of the guys happened by and found him skulking around. The pits. Yanking his stuff off the hooks, he picked up the helmet—it wasn't really his, but he couldn't leave it here with all those personal stars on it. If the school had a gripe, Clint would field it. Right now, cut the chalk-talk.

Rain was coming down when he stepped back out into the night. Gritty little pellets of sleet pecked at his face as he fumbled with the keys and—why won't the stupid trunk unlock?

Shucking his load into the back seat, he got out the Big Beam and took it around to the rear, where its pale cone revealed scratches, as if the trunk had been jimmied. If some jerk lifted my spare—

Forcing the key harder, Scott finally got it to turn. As the lid rose on its spring, he stared blankly at the figure folded awkwardly inside. A wax dummy? He shifted the light to the face, which was vaguely familiar. It sort of resembled that G-man, Holdrege. Right down to the Band-Aid under his chin . . .

Scott stumbled backward, sweat breaking out. As the rain dripped off his hair, he swung the flashlight wildly, but the parking lot was an island of emptiness. Anyway, he hadn't been inside long enough for anyone to stow a— It had to be earlier, while he was at dinner maybe? His belly lumped up like a clenched fist.

With his eyes anywhere else, Scott slammed the trunk lid. Couldn't think with It staring at him. He ought to get rid of the thing, but the idea of touching It made him almost come violently unstuck. He swallowed hard. Again. Then slung himself into the front seat and gripped the wheel with both hands.

Got to be a mistake. A bad joke. Except jokes don't get that bad.

Maybe he's not completely dead. Sure, he's lying there with his eyes open, waiting for the second half to start.

By why? Who? "Who" is probably those voices you heard. "Why" is, you tried to finger them, they found out, and are returning the favor.

Found out how? Who knows? Maybe they saw your car in the lot that night. Everyone in town could tell them who owns a red Mustang. Then they could have tailed you to Holdrege's office—never mind. Question is: What do I do now? Go to the cops? And tell them—what? The truth is too far out. Nobody would believe this!

From the distance, as if he'd dreamed them up, Scott heard sirens. And the rest of the picture came on like Insta-Cam. Whoever did it, they didn't wait for me to think up explanations. Anonymous phone call, and the law's on its way to your house. Where your mother will kindly tell them you're over at school.

Beyond the stadium a glitter of brilliance came and went—white, red, blue, slashing the wet darkness like a scream. Picture in the paper: "Son of prominent oil man arrested on suspicion of murder."

No. His hands had started the car, the motor was humming. Without headlights, he steered cautiously out of the lot, watching the mirror. Turning away from the flashers, he moved blacked-out down an avenue flanked by tall elderly houses, one of which he recognized. Memory of a tea party, Freshman English "get-acquainted" thing, years ago. Not his favorite recollection. All that mattered now, the front windows were dark. Swinging into the driveway, he cut the engine.

Gotta figure out what to do. Slumped low in the seat, he hoped the night would eat up the red of the Mustang. He hoped the rain would pour bull yearlings, horns down'ard. Most of all, he hoped Miss McGill had gone to bed early.

ISABELL

❏

WHY? SHE wondered. What sniggering Fate decreed that gray hair shall clump at a man's temples, giving him a touch of distinction, while in a woman's hair it threads out all over the place to render her drab? Leaning closer to the bathroom mirror, Isabell McGill singled out the offending strand and prepared to pluck it. Then hesitated.

Maybe it was exactly what she needed to put more iron in her image. Even after eleven years in front of a classroom, she was still devising disguises, biting back the girlish smile, camouflaging the sensitive hazel eyes behind steel-rimmed glasses, tucking the dark brown masses of hair into a bun that was pure cliché. Peering into the mirror, she checked for blackheads. Kids were quick to grade you—D for dowdiness, F for fear. They smell it and they track you. So you try to look like a gargoyle and sound like God, reminding yourself desperately that God doesn't make mistakes.

From the dark master bedroom at the front of the house

came the ghostly echo of a snort. The Major's vibrations still haunted her. "I told you, girl, it takes a wealth of inner strength to be a teacher."

You also implied I didn't have it. Isabell could still see the contempt in his bulldogged face, scorn for the daughter who should have been a son. It was a portrait that hung in the attic of her mind like an unwanted antique. No matter how often she told herself it had all ended four years ago with a military funeral, she could still feel her father's presence in that room. She hated to enter it.

But the rain was racking the house, rattling the windows. She had to be sure the front ones were fastened tight. Going quickly along the hall, she went in without turning on the lights. A cold draft was coming from somewhere. Or maybe she was just shivering at the thought of another long winter. Have to get out the heavy clothes. *In six-and-a-half more flannel nightgowns I will be forty years old.* Shoving the curtains aside, she checked the window lock—and stopped short. A car in the driveway?

It looked like Scott Drummond's Mustang. Always a distinctive spot of color in the school parking lot, she had rather applauded it, the bright scarlet of youth, the chrome of self-confidence. Now, it looked almost furtive out there in the shadows.

It brought back that scene in the hospital when she had visited the boy, only to find a stranger. Those powerfully muscled limbs lying listless, blond hair plastered to a damp brow, eyes tarnished with despair—this was not the young man who had looked so staunchly from the cover of that sports magazine last fall, tallest of the group of quarterbacks, captioned: "High School's Super Six." Only a few months ago one of the chosen athletes from around the country, and now, defeated. When he'd glanced at her distantly it was with a look that stood her heart on end with recognition. So much like another young face in torment! A time she couldn't bear to remember . . . when she'd got her voice back she'd heard herself babbling a lot of stupid teacher-talk while her mind rang with a different cry: Not *again?*

And this one she was even less prepared for. She didn't know Scott the way she had known Fernando. To call up that name sent her into a cramp she had to fight to break. Maybe that's why she had cut the visit short, trying to avoid involvement. Telling herself that Scott would be all right, he's a survivor, he has a loving family and money is no problem. Inventing reasons for not worrying about him. *How could I have been so cowardly?*

And now the problem was sitting out there in a darkened car, telegraphing a message—trying to get up the nerve to come in, but too shy to make the first move. Rushing back to her room, Isabell rummaged for the heavy turtleneck sweater. Earlier she had put on a pair of wool slacks to ward off the chill. Now she kicked off her slippers and hauled on waterproof walking shoes. Because this time she was going to proceed with caution. Don't force it. Be casual, stand out in the rain a while if necessary. Slipping into the all-weather coat, she ran down the stairs. No, don't put the porch light on; obviously he feels more at ease in the dark. For God's sake, don't blow it!

Pulling up the hood of the coat, she stepped out into the night. The shadowy silhouette in the car seemed to hunch lower. Venturing up to the far side where the window was rolled down an inch, she said, "Scott? Are you all right?"

"Oh, hi, Miss McGill. Sorry if I woke you up. I just pulled in here a minute to—you know—think." Voice thin with stress.

"Why don't you come inside and get warm? I'll make us some coffee."

"No! I mean, thanks, but no thanks. I really ought to be heading home." His breath steamed on the cold air. "You're getting all wet. You better go back in the house, okay?"

Walk away? Lose contact? No, you have to stay close at all risk. "You're right, it sure is raining hard." Quickly she opened the car door and slid in beside him. "Scott, thinking is great. But sometimes talking can be even better. I'm a good listener."

Startled, he seemed at a loss for words. Then, in a rush, he said, "Miss McGill, I'm sorry I bothered you. I needed a place to park for a minute, but now I really have to get going." He kept glancing over his shoulders as if the vultures were circling. And for the first time Isabell became aware of the colored flashers of a police unit cruising over on the next block. They seemed to be searching yards with a powerful spotlight.

"Scott, are you in trouble with the law?"

"No. NO! Of course not." He gave an odd high-pitched laugh. "Well, say, I'd better get home, Mom will be worrying. It was nice to see you." He started the engine. "Miss McGill, please!"

And from the far distances within her, Fernando yelled, "Get off my case!"

"Would you?" she asked calmly. "Would you turn your back on someone in trouble?"

The boy beat the wheel with his fist in obvious frustration. Peering along the street, he suddenly sent the Mustang backward out of the driveway. She saw that the police car had turned the corner a few blocks down and was heading this way. At the next intersection Scott swung left, steering by the light of the streetlamps that hung like furry beacons suspended in the downpour. Windshield wipers slashing, he raced a fast block through the dark and turned right, heading away from town toward a lot of nowhere off to the west. When they reached the frontage road, he braked abruptly.

"Miss McGill, you've got to get out. Right now. Better you should get wet than go any farther with me." In the dim dashboard light, the young face was haggard.

"Scott, listen: Whatever is wrong, it will work itself out more easily if I'm along. I can be a great buffer. The police will be more inclined to listen to reason if I'm with you."

Another rack of flashers was coming along from the south. Scott swore and swung the wheel over, swerving onto a county secondary. Using only fog lights, they rattled over washboard with gravel kicking up like buckshot against the bottoms of the fenders. As the car jolted in and out of potholes, a whole circus of spinning brilliance clustered back at the intersection.

"I think they saw us," he groaned. "You should have got out while you could."

"And leave you to cope with this trouble by yourself? I care too much about you to do that." Isabell spoke flatly to rob the statement of sentimentality. But he gave no sign of having heard.

Once they had reached the folds of high country, he pulled on his long beams—the rain hurled them back at him. Then, abruptly, it changed to a smothering eiderdown of white that cut visibility to a few feet. On instinct alone, the boy sent the car shearing through the stuff headlong, his agile hands whipping the wheel as if the vehicle were an extension of himself, hipswitching to avoid the deep ruts, jinking up onto a shoulder past a muddy spot, shrugging off the snatch of low branches as they hurtled through the dense forest.

Hands clamped tight in her lap, Isabell felt the seed of panic. In all that silence, it was taking hold. Trying to speak calmly, she said, "You seem to know these hills fairly well."

"Like my own backyard." He veered onto a narrow track to avoid the highest part of the Plateau, racing down a small canyon and across a rickety fisherman's bridge. "Me and Clint come up here every summer. For years. Camp out. Mess around. He taught me how to tie flies, he taught me everything. My father is a great guy!" It burst out angry and defensive, for reasons she couldn't even guess. "I bet I know the roads better than those cops back there."

"The police? Oh, I doubt they'd try to follow you through this snow," she remarked. "They'll just radio your license number on ahead to the Utah State Patrol."

Swerving violently, Scott brought the car to a halt. "Damn it! Why did you have to go think of that?"

"Well, it's a good thing one of us is considering the possibilities. Now we're stopped, why don't we look at your options? We're safe for the moment."

Still gripping the wheel, Scott sat hunched, a small sound escaping like a kettle on the boil. His shoulders shook. "One lousy night, me and Miss McGill, went for a drive, over the hill . . ." His head dropped helplessly onto the wheel as he convulsed with laughter.

"I grant you, it's a bit weird." She forced a chuckle. "I'd like to enjoy the joke too, but I can't until you tell me the rest of it."

"You know what's really funny?" He was on the verge

of hysteria. "I suddenly got it, the perfect scam! If . . . if cops stop us now . . . I'll tell 'em you're . . . my hostage! If I can be killer . . . you can be . . . hostage. Cinch!"

In her icy corner, Isabell tittered like an uncertain echo. Dear God, the boy has gone completely around the bend. Out in the middle of the Uncompahgre, snowing, night, the nearest phone miles away. And anyhow I don't have any change. Drat it, I came off without my purse.

ISABELL

[ii]

❑

IN EDUCATION 101, there should be at least a semester devoted to faces. Mysterious as uncharted waters. In a schoolroom they take on a surface brightness like a string of ponds at sunrise, revealing nothing but reflected image: Class Clown. Serious Student. Glamour Girl. Jock.

Isabell winced at the word now, as she glanced up at this man/boy/stranger striding along beside her in the bleached light of dawn. An uncomplicated kid who used to sit third-row-next-to-the-last-on-the-left, now his face was shaded with infinite depths of complexity. And no wonder.

This story he'd told her, after he'd got himself back in control and they'd traveled on through the night—it was almost incredible. And yet he had recounted it with such amazing clarity, such total recall, it confirmed her long-held opinion that the boy had an excellent mind if he'd only use it for something other than a football chalkboard.

Not fair, she amended the thought. Those playing fields

have given him the strength to haul himself back from the edge of chaos. Coolness under pressure—that didn't surprise her. What did was his concern for her.

In the midst of his own turmoil he'd kept her in mind. "We've got to figure a way to get you back home. If you're with me when the law catches up, they might say you are, like, an accessory. To murder."

"I can't believe— I'm finding it hard to accept all this," she admitted. "Maybe if I could look at the—"

"No!"

They had abandoned the Mustang in a clearing before they reached the edge of the forest. Scott had been firm about leaving the trunk unopened. "Maybe I'll say the car got stolen, I never did know about any dead body."

"They'll ask, in that case, why did you run?" She said, "Scott, each lie is going to mire you deeper and make you look guiltier. I really think your best bet is to go back and tell the truth."

"But the truth doesn't make any sense." With a touch of desperation. "The people who wanted me in the sheep-dip set this up good. They must have made a phone call to the sheriff, or the police—doesn't matter, they work together. 'Hey, guess what—I saw old Drummer stash a corpse in his car.' How could I prove I didn't? If I go to jail, my folks will be hung out to dry—well, you know Twin Forks. Little town, being in jail you never get over the stink of. Vanishing is better, there's not much for the papers to write about. No, I'm not going back."

So now they walked in silence down out of the cold hills. But the snow was already melting on the road, and it never had reached the lowland. They had come through the mountains and out onto a long slope leading down to a rocky valley that stretched north and south like a giant dry riverbed. Bounded on the west by a ragged barrier of rimrock, the empty land was dotted with a few meager farms and ranches. Only a hard-working people like the Mormons could have made a living off it, Isabell thought, watching a distant milk truck move along the highway that sliced it down the middle.

Without breaking stride, Scott was counting through a fistful of bills. "You got any money on you?"

"Not a cent."

"I think I have enough to buy you a bus ticket home."

"Stop worrying about me. We need to focus on a plan of action. I still believe our safest course is to go to the police."

"Look," he said impatiently, "how do I know who's who? Somebody went to a lot of trouble to frame me. I keep wondering why. What if they wanted me picked up, so they could take care of me legally, say I was trying to escape, had to shoot, and like that? I don't mind dying, but not as a notch on some cop's gun. There're better ways to go." He spoke with a morbid humor that made Isabell quake right down to the core, recalling Fernando's sad, brash grin: "Nobody lives forever, Teach."

"I hadn't thought of that," she said. "It is extremely odd—that you should happen to be at the right place and time to hear the vital details of an international bomb plot."

"And the very guy I talked to about it turns up dead. In the trunk of *my* car."

"Did anyone follow you to his office? Did you tell anyone you were going there?"

He shook his head.

"Anyone hanging around when you left?"

"Half the people on earth heard me leave. I was mad. I was yelling at him, the dumb jerk, he kept putting me down, you know. So I said, like, 'Don't be too shocked if you wake up dead.' "

Isabell stumbled, a chuckhole. Scott caught her arm and steadied her. For a while they walked in silence. But the sense of incongruity kept growing. "The only way I can make heads or tails of it," she said at last, "is if someone targeted you right from the start. Followed you to the stadium and threw out the bait—"

"On purpose, so I'd go to the FBI and they could murder Holdrege and pack him into my trunk when I wasn't looking and sic the cops onto me. But why would anybody go to that much trouble? As far as I know I don't have an enemy in the world."

Isabell believed it. She had no answers, but she was beginning to perceive the dimensions of something very deadly indeed. Glancing up at him in the first thin light of the sun, it struck her: Once we get out of these hills that boy is going to stand out in a crowd like Jason looking for the fleece. Pulling off her steel-rim specs, she handed them to him. "Put these on."

Scott seemed puzzled, then got the idea and did as she asked. A slight grin uncrimped his lips. "These are plain glass."

"Classroom camouflage," she confessed. "They do help change your looks. We can't shrink you, but you might wear the fishing cap." It had been drizzling when they left the car, he'd slapped the old canvas hat on his head, but when the sky cleared, he'd stuffed it in his pocket. Now he put it on and turned the reversible Mackinaw inside-out. The lining was red lumberjack plaid that added twenty pounds to his weight. Slumping, he began to plod slowly as if on sore feet. "Do I look like a skunked hunter?"

"Not bad. And I'd better be your old aunt who came along to pluck the ducks. Because right now there is a vehicle approaching behind us."

"I know. I heard it back there." He turned wearily and stuck out a thumb.

BY MIDMORNING the last shreds of cloud had blown off to the east, leaving a bright sky, clean as the inside of an icebox. "I wish this guy had been heading south." Scott's words shivered away on the breeze.

Even though the coat was sturdy, Isabell felt the cut of the wind, as they perched on the back of the pickup with their feet just above the skimming blacktop. She glanced at the spot on her wrist where her watch usually reassured her that this-too-shall-pass. Another item from a different life. She pictured the old house getting warm as the thermostat took over. The Major's spectre would be stalking the empty rooms, grunting with irritation. "Trouble with you, m'dear, you feel you have to carry the weight of the world on your shoulders and they really aren't built for it." And the old man was right, she hadn't done too well last time, failed miserably. But now she had a second chance if she could just get her head together before it was too late.

Turning to Scott, she asked, "Do you have the time?"

"Ten thirty-seven. You hungry too?"

When you're young you have such appetites. Then the zest for living dies down and hunger becomes another bodily function. And yet, it dawned on Isabell, for the first time in years she could remember suddenly what it felt like—to be ravenous. "We should reach town soon. These people are obviously headed for church."

The rawboned rancher and his wife were dressed in their Sunday clothes, but their manners were natural as daily bread. "Need a ride? Saw your car back there in the woods, too bad. We can take you in to Moab."

That was an hour ago. Now they were slowing to a stop in front of a large truck depot. Leaning out the window, the man called back. "Ask for Porter Scofield. Whatever's broke in your car he can fix. Good luck." And the pickup was rattling off down the highway toward a small town—rows of houses held slightly aloof from a main drag of stores and motels.

As they began to walk toward it, Scott said, too casually, "Reckon they'll be expecting us?"

"Certainly not two of us. Anyway, a town this size can't have a very large police force. Let's hope they hold off until we get something to eat." Her inner compass had swung toward the flicker of a Cafe sign.

He heaved a sigh. "Trouble is, if I buy us breakfast I won't have enough for your bus ticket."

"I told you, I'm not jumping ship."

"But Gilly—" He broke off sheepishly.

"It's all right. I know the kids call me that, I don't mind. We may as well be informal, because you're stuck with me until we resolve this situation. But we can't think on 'empty.'"

A bluff. She couldn't think, period. She hadn't a clue to a logical course of action—the realization shocked Isabell deeply. All these years of paper problems had left her with total faith in solutions. There had to be one, didn't there? If only she could shake the daze of unreality—to place herself here in Moab, Utah, a fugitive from the law, tearing into the ham and eggs like a lumberjack. Scott was devouring his platter of hotcakes and sausage mechanically, as if he were fueling a machine.

"I've got to call Mom so she won't worry. Only whatever I say is going to worry her more." The steel-rimmed glasses gave him a silly ineffectual look. Isabell suddenly wondered if she'd been wrong to hide behind them all these years.

"The sound of your voice would be enough," she assured him. "And she may be able to help. Maybe she could get hold of a lawyer who will listen to your story and stand by you if you give yourself up?"

He considered this, the young face lightening a bit. "You know, it might work. Clint may be back from Oklahoma now—he knows a lot of state senators and stuff. Let's go find a pay phone." But as they walked out of the restaurant the sight of the sheriff's cruiser parked on the next block sent him veering down a side street. She had to trot to keep up.

"Lousy idea," he muttered. "I don't want the folks involved in this." He was gravitating toward a small park with a playground where kids swarmed all over a battered slide. Parents and idlers huddled in heavy coats watching in the feeble sunlight. Scott found a bench near the swings and slung himself onto it.

Isabell understood—they were somewhat less noticeable here. But it was not a place she would have chosen to think out a plan of action. And to compound her frustration, now an old man was ambling toward them. Shabby clothes topped by a scrap of tarpaulin around his shoulders, uncombed dirty hair sprouting like straw from under a seedy hat, he sang to himself in a high-pitched toneless mutter. As he sank down onto their bench, Scott stirred, ready to get up. The bum gave them a toothless grin, mopping his face with a red kerchief. And strangely, from behind it came a low voice, even, articulate, edged with authority.

"Stay where you are. Turn away from me, and listen."

Isabell opened her mouth, then shut it as she saw a change come over the boy, a stiffening of recognition. He obviously recognized those level tones. His face was undone by shock and, curiously, relief.

"You're being followed," the quiet words went on. "Swarthy man, thirties, stocky. Ring any bells?"

"No, sir," Scott muttered.

Cautiously Isabell glanced around and saw him—fifty feet away on another bench, an Indian. The bone structure was strongly Athabascan, probably a Navajo. But dressed like an easterner in buttoned-down business clothes.

"You've got to shake him." Then as some people came past, the derelict leaned back and began to sing in an aged, listless quaver . . . "tell you why I fwy by night, 'cause I lost m'heart's dewight . . ." The toothless slurring of the words trailed off and the low voice said, "When I leave, wait three minutes. Go back to the place where you ate. Down the hall and out the back door, find a white pickup in the alley, keys on the sun visor. Drive south two blocks, Golden Beehive Motel, room nineteen, key's on the dash. Wait there." Then the old man rose, scratching himself in the dispirited way of the alcoholic and doddered off toward the public comfort station.

Scott was struggling visibly with his face.

"I think," Isabell told him dryly, "a little amusement would only be natural."

And he exploded like a held breath, snorting, choking. She joined in the act—the Indian was glancing over at them. When she sensed it was enough she said under her breath, "So now what?"

[40]

"Now, we follow orders like crazy and thank the Lord he's here." Scott was still grinning furiously. "Only how did he find us?"

"You mean you know that old wino?"

He shook his head, threatening to break up again. "Not personally. But I know who he is. I think . . . I th-th-think he's my . . . long lost . . . daddy."

JONAH

❑

CLEAN REST room. Forgot how sanitary small-town USA can be. Or tries to be—ten-year-olds at the urinals, never quite accurate, giggle and gone before they're zipped. Nobody else around, nobody in the stalls. Relax. Open the window a crack, watch what the two are doing . . . still sitting there . . .

Now. She's pretending she lost her purse: we have to go back to the Cafe. Pretty good. Who is she, this woman? Anyway she's got all her smarts.

The boy, too—my son!

Put a lid on that and keep it screwed down. Watch the Indian—there he goes, trying to look invisible. In those big-city duds he stands out like a walnut in a bowl of marshmallows. No technique. With any luck they'll lose him.

Talk about walnuts, my own image stinks. This is no town for a wino. What'd you bet somebody's already gone for the law? Good thing it's Sunday, cops off duty. Time to move on, though.

Several of those proper citizens keeping their eye on this building, going to remember the old bum. Rags are easy to shed, but the face— Take some toilet paper. Blow the nose as you step on out. Good, they turn away. Be disgusting in a civilized world, you disappear.

All the same, better double around the block. Could be somebody out there better trained than the Indian. Head for the main drag, around another corner and hitch a hip on one of the railings of the Far West Trading Post (closed). See who shows up. Sit in the sun and think.

Indulge it now or it may swamp you suddenly later when you don't need it. Think about the kid.

Pictures never do justice, they don't capture that spirit. Keen. Quick. Adjust to a situation—how fast he accepted it. Followed orders, no question. Probably the football training. Did that teach him to keep on functioning in a whirlwind of confusion? Hard thing to learn, maybe he comes by it naturally. Anger in those young eyes, he senses he's been used, even if he doesn't know how or why. Fighting to keep his options open, until he can figure it out. Fast on his feet. My son.

Don't break your arm patting your own back, buddy, you didn't contribute. All the honors go to Helene. Great girl. Highbred like a pedigreed filly, trained for the show ring, not the rough rodeo of life. After all these years, still see her face as young and delicate and twenty-one. Haven't got any recent snaps.

The newer pictures have all been of the boy. Fresh batch every fall, football season the PI sends clips from the Twin Forks *Gazette*. Bet they'd be surprised to find their sports pages decorating a basement hideout in Beirut, Lebanon.

A good hole beneath a bombed-out building, even my own squad doesn't know about it. Not because I don't trust 'em, but a man needs some privacy. Scraps of normality. To hang up a few pictures and remember you once used to be human. Remember . . .

Hold it. Car turned the corner, go into your act. "Reason why I fwy by night is 'cause I wost my heart's dewight . . ." Moving on past, full of rigid Mormon faces that stare, then turn away. No sweat, Saints, I'm out of here.

Time to check up on the scheme. Down the next side street, and what if the room at the motel is empty? Deal with that if and when. Here's the alley and—there's the white pickup at the far end. Good boy. Parked out of sight of the street, smart kid. Damn them for harassing him this way to get to me!

Stow that. Head for the pickup. Old Ford with a low camper shell, dents and rust and a bumper sticker: WELCOME TO COLORADO—NOW GO HOME! Extremely suitable.

Lucky to find it so fast, last night; an hour after my jet hit the runway at Grand Junction I've got wheels. Early edition of the Sunday paper—widow wanted to unload it. Didn't even want to clean her husband's junk out of the back, regular rat's nest of odds and ends. Handy to rig a disguise in a hurry, when I saw that Indian.

Almost too much luck to pick up the trail just as the two of them headed into the eatery. Gave me a half-hour to get in place and character. But I've got to shed it now.

I'm not walking into that room without at least putting my dentures back in.

SCOTT

COINCIDENCES HE hated. With everything already gone ding-dong, he didn't need the yellow Toyota.

The minute he saw it parked there, two doors down, Scott retreated to the bathroom to think: Was it there when I drove in? Can't remember, don't think so. Maybe Buford's shadowing me too? Or had the guy just come over to Utah to hit up the Mormons for his fund raising? If so, why this motel? There must have been a dozen better ones around town. Hard to picture the man as sinister. Terrorists don't come in size double-dumpling, they don't wear bifocals—ruins your aim with those sniper scopes. All the same, coincidences . . .

He was standing there, studying the shower curtain for clues, when a few inches from his left elbow the window moved a fraction. The security device had been removed—Scott saw it on the flush box and got the picture.

Swallowing the frogs that had jumped up in his throat, he said, "Come on in. It's only me here."

"Thanks." The casement was shoved aside, the man in the alley swung himself up and in with a single lithe movement like an acrobat. Tough, taller, younger, Jonah was dressed in jeans and a black jersey. Face still crusted with dirt, he headed for the shower, picking up one of the dinky motel soap bars, tearing off the wrapper. "When I set up a bathroom entrance I didn't figure on a woman around. Always some fool thing you neglect to factor in."

"That 'fool thing' happens to be my friend." Scott was shocked at his own surly tone. But being confused always made him mad. When a guy's image keeps changing—

"Looks like you shook the tail." Pike stuck his head under the hot water, lathering his hair roughly. A lot of grease and grit down the drain. When he turned around, the face that emerged from the folds of the towel looked about forty, cheeks like hardwood, grooved with stress lines. Reminded Scott of some actor—the one that played the ruined song-and-dance man who kept dying in *All That Jazz*. Only how did he change the mouth? Now it was firm as a hard fact.

"You got false choppers!"

Jonah looked amused. "Lost my own in a Turkish prison years ago. At the time I regretted it, but it's come in handy." They stood eyeing each other as if both had the same thought: This wasn't the way they had pictured their first meeting.

"Before we go in there"—the older man was picking his words more carefully this time—"you ought to know that this business could get sticky. Are you sure you want to involve the lady?"

"No. No, of course not! But I can't get her to go home," Scott blurted. "She's a schoolteacher."

"Okay if I try?"

[46]

"Be my guest." He followed into the bedroom where Gilly sat hunched in front of the TV.

"I thought there might be some local news—" Then she saw Jonah. Leaping to her feet, she slicked her hair back and put on her glasses. Stepping forward, brisk as if this was sixth-hour study hall, she held out her hand. "I'm Isabell McGill."

"Jonah Pike." He gave it a brief shake. "I want to thank you for standing by my son when he was in trouble. Now, though, I can take over. I'm sure you want to get back to Twin Forks before people start to worry about you."

Scott stood in for an assist. "Really, Miss McGill, I'll be okay."

Giving Jonah a hard look, the one the kids called her "weevil eye," she said, "This whole chain of events is very strange, and you know exactly what it's all about, don't you? Suppose you fill us in."

"You're right, it's complicated and it only concerns me and the boy. We don't want to put you in further danger. So if you'd catch the next bus—"

"I'll decide what I'm going to do after you tell me more about it." She sat down on the bed like forever.

Scott sank onto the other one. If he knew old Gilly, she wasn't going to give up.

Jonah seemed to read her chin, too. He pulled a chair around and straddled it backward. "I can tell you some of it. To begin, you have to know that the talk under the bleachers was undoubtedly staged. Obviously nobody is going to blither around about bombs in a small-town stadium at midnight."

"We managed to figure that out," Gilly informed him. "Let's get to who and why. Why use Scott to spread word of a nonexistent plot?"

[47]

"Oh, the plot is real enough." Jonah made a gesture with the long hands draped over the back of the chair. A thin set of matching scars ran across the fingers of the left. "A gang of global terrorists is planning to create synchronized havoc around the world next New Year's Eve. The exact details aren't known yet, even by the CIA. They undoubtedly made up a lot of that, about arenas and stadiums, to provide a good story for the boy to hear and report."

Hold it, *hold it!* Scott said, "Are you telling us the Company put on that show?"

"I'd bet my last nickel on it. They figured you or your mother would have a way of reaching me. If you'd tried to go directly to them, they'd have laughed you off. They undoubtedly cued the FBI to give you the brush so you'd have to turn to me. Don't sweat it, you did exactly right. I got the message: they know I have a son."

"You mean they didn't know that?" Scott marveled.

"I thought I'd kept it a total secret. Why else do you think I kept so much distance between us? I didn't even want to risk phone calls."

Scott didn't get it and Gilly looked puzzled.

With visible patience Jonah explained. "Nineteen years ago, on a skiing vacation, I met a beautiful girl and we were married very anonymously. I didn't use my real name. I was determined the Company shouldn't know about her—they're perfectly capable of using people for leverage like any other secret police. And as soon as she told me I was going to be a father, I realized the whole thing was a bad mistake. I arranged for her to get a Caribbean divorce—we went to great lengths to cover it all up. I still don't know how they found out. But now, as I said, they're using it, a subtle form of blackmail to get me to come in."

"Why are they after you?" Gilly demanded bluntly.

"Several reasons. Mainly because I'm ahead of them in a manhunt. Terrorism is a murderous sickness that's spreading across the world. The civilized countries can't fight it properly because their agencies are hampered by red tape, bureaucrats, diplomats, foreign policy. It's why I quit the CIA and formed my own team of the best ex-operatives from all parts of the world. We work without a leash and we're beginning to succeed. The Company knows this; they want to bring me in and learn my sources, tap my intelligence banks, adapt my operations to their own purposes."

"Why not cooperate? You're all after the same thing."

"I don't like the constrictions, as I said. And for another thing, I had an idea they've been infiltrated by the other side. Our boys wouldn't kill an FBI man. I've suspected for some time that the headquarters at Langley have been penetrated, which means some anarchist is feeding back every step of the Company's plans. It also means they know about my son too, these lawless scumbags, and if they could get their hands on him, they'd try to use him to flush me out. My team is causing them lots of grief right now. They'd love to upset its quarterback."

Scott could buy that.

But Gilly still had her suspicions. "The more you tell me, the more I believe your son would be safer in jail."

Jonah squeezed out a few more drops of patience. Very distinctly he said, "If the terrorists want him in jail, then I do *not* want him there. If they can hit the FBI, they can certainly bribe the guard in a small-town slam. Snatch my son and they've got me by the short hairs, which I do not intend to let happen. International espionage is a rough game, Miss McGill, so will you do us all a favor and—"

"Leave Scott here in this free-fire zone? With a man he doesn't even know? I think not." She was pale, but determined.

"I'll be okay, Gilly," Scott pleaded. "Please go home."

When she turned to him, the color rushed back to her cheekbones as she said, "I can't do that. *I can't.*" And for some reason she meant a whole lot of "can't" that he didn't understand. "Anyway, we don't seem to be in much danger for the moment. We lost the Indian—I don't even believe he was following us. Who would know we were here? How would they find out?"

"The same way I did," Jonah told her. "The minute I got here I bought a police scanner. And the first squawk I caught was about a kid in Twin Forks wanted for murder, last seen heading west through the Uncompahgre. Did you think you were invisible? Or that people don't have maps? This is the only town west of the mountains for fifty miles around. I'd give odds the FBI is sending a whole troop. They tend to get touchy when one of their agents is killed. The CIA may already be on the scene. The informer at Langley has surely sent word to the terrorists. Soon half the spies on earth are going to be elbowing each other around Moab, Utah."

Maybe driving yellow Toyotas? Foggy with exhaustion, Scott wondered if he'd better mention it. But by then the old body was taking over. He tipped quietly onto the pillow, had to get his head down just for a minute . . .

SCOTT

[ii]

❏

HE WAKENED out of a familiar dream: the ball was stuck to his hand, a receiver was already downfield and he could not—turn loose of—the crazy— Struggling awake, Scott could hardly get his fingers unclenched.

Or his mind. Over by the window some man stood as if on watch. It took long seconds to make the connection, that this was actually his father.

Jonah glanced across at him. "Morning."

All night? I've missed a whole night?

"Where's Gilly?" He struggled up to sit on the side of the bed.

"Gone out to get coffee. How do you feel?"

For some reason the question hit a raw spot. Scott couldn't help it—all these years the guy hasn't worried how I feel, does he think I'm some kind of weakling just because I sacked out pretty hard?

"I feel like hitting the road," he said. "Let's split while she's gone."

"It occurred to me," Jonah remarked in that toneless voice, "but she took the keys to the truck. Must have lifted them when she put the blanket over you last night."

Scott felt through his pockets—everybody on earth had gone through his pockets. Sorely he hauled himself up off the bed and went in to shower. The hot water steamed away some of the thickness—it all came back to him, the park yesterday, coming here, learning some of the reasons behind all this. Mostly, one thing kept sticking to his mind like Velcro, what Jonah had said. *He and Mom made out all right until I came along.* And then it hit him—Mom! She must be going out of her skull about now!

Throwing on clothes, Scott hurried back to the bedroom. "I've got to call home."

"I took care of that," Jonah told him. "Your mother knows you're okay and with me."

"Maybe she'd like to hear it in person." Scott was headed for the phone when Jonah held up the hand with those scarred fingers.

"I think her line's been tapped. The bug gives off a slight hum."

"What difference? If you talked to her, the whole world knows where we are."

"I don't think so. I used an old code that she and I once concocted back in the early days. She still remembered it." You'd almost think the hardness of that face eased up a little. There was a twitch that could have turned into a smile if he'd let it.

"What code?" Scott asked in spite of himself. He had sworn when he was about eight years old that he would never again ask questions about the time when his mother was married to the unknown man who had fathered him. She wouldn't—or maybe she couldn't—answer any of them anyway. All these years, the only thing he really knew was that the guy had walked out on them the way you leave when a movie gets boring. So he hated to admit, now, that he was slightly curious.

Jonah hitched one shoulder as if it was no big deal. "It concerned a basket of fruit she'd ordered. She's the oranges, I'm grapefruit. The bad guys are pistachio nuts, which are hanging all over the trees right now."

"And what am I, some kind of—"

"Apples. Well, I figured you're the apple of her eye. Must say she caught onto it fast. I promised her I would deliver all items in prime condition once I have picked the pistachios." He turned back to the window and stiffened. "Now what?"

Coming to look over his shoulder, Scott saw Gilly walking up the driveway of the motel, carrying a sack and towing a younger woman who was hanging onto her arm.

"Why would she pick up some stranger?" Scott couldn't believe it.

"Or maybe she was the one picked up. She's walking slow to give us a chance to clear out." Jonah headed for the rear.

Scott hung there a minute by the window. "Wait. I know that girl. She's from Twin Forks—archaeologist. She's okay, she likes football."

"That hardly gives her security clearance. Come on."

"But Gilly may need help getting rid of her."

"All right, wait if you want. But don't under any circumstances mention me, you got that?" His father disappeared into the bathroom.

Scott opened the door and waved to Gilly: Come on in, coast's clear.

The girl didn't even notice, she sounded half-hysterical.

" . . . never so glad in my life! Only you still didn't tell me what you're doing here, Miss McGill. Aren't classes still on over in Twin Forks? Or did you quit? I bet you quit, you always were too good for that—" Then she saw Scott and her mouth went "Oh."

"Hi." He gave her a grin he hoped was nonhorrible. Obviously she knew who he was by now. As he stood back to let them in, she gave him a slightly crooked smile like, *hello, I think*. She seemed cuter than he remembered, with the brown curls messed up across her forehead and the little bobbed nose looking very brave.

Miss McGill was trying to invent fiction. "We came over on a field trip and got separated from the rest and the bus went off and left us and—you know better, don't you, dear? Scott, this is Beth Frawley, one of my former students. We ran into each other in the coffee shop. Oh, here's the coffee, you'd better take it in the bathroom to open it, so it won't slop onto the rug."

Quick thinking, because there were three cups of java and three doughnuts in the sack. In the john, he silently gave one of each to Jonah, who was poised behind the door, listening. Taking the other two back, he handed one to Beth.

"Have mine. You look like you need it. I—uh—guess my picture made the *Gazette*, right?"

She nodded silently.

"Well, if you think I could kill anybody, forget it. I was framed."

She nodded more vigorously. "I'm sure of that. I mean the paper said you were seen putting a—a—dead body in your car late Saturday afternoon. But you were at the football game, so how could you? Unless—" she flushed and took a bite of doughnut.

[54]

"Unless what?"

"Well, I suppose it's barely possible you went off, got into a snit and rapidly killed somebody right after the game." In spite of herself she giggled.

"Yeah, and then went home and had a quiet dinner with my mother and a friend." When you thought about it, the whole thing was silly.

"Listen," Beth sobered down, "why don't I go with you to the police? I was about to look them up anyway when I ran into Miss McGill. Someone has been following me!" The wide blue eyes were bright as lake water with ripples of returning fear. "Ever since yesterday. I went out to see the Arches Monument in the afternoon and when I got back, I noticed this man. He kept turning up wherever I went—the restaurant, my motel. This morning when I was eating breakfast, there he was again. That's when I sort of grabbed Miss McGill. I mean it's scary!"

"What kind of man?" Scott thought he already knew.

"An Indian. Either a Navajo or an Apache, wouldn't you say, Miss McGill? She knows more about Indians than I do. She's the main reason I went into archaeology—she was the sponsor for our Stone-Hunter Club, back in high school, always spinning such marvelous tales about the Anasazi and Folsom man . . ."

"This guy"—he tried to calm her nervous babble—"he's not really after you. He's been on my tail, I don't know how long. If he was hanging around the game the other day he may have seen us together. So when I got away from him, he latched onto you, hoping you'd lead him to me."

Alarm flared in her eyes. "Which I did! Oh, I'm sorry!"

"I think we gave him the slip." Gilly peered through the window curtains. "I steered us through the park and around a couple of blocks. I think we lost him. Unless, of course, he's out in back. I can see that better from the bathroom." She went in there, closing the door behind her.

"But why is he after you?" Beth wondered.

"Who knows?" Scott steered away from a quiz session. "Why aren't you down in Arizona by now?"

"I wanted to see the country on the way. There are a number of petroglyphs over in the Canyonlands. But I'd hate to go off on those lonely roads with a—a—"

"Yeah."

"So let's do go to the police. I can tell them you weren't killing anybody Saturday afternoon, and they'll pick up this Indian, at least hold onto him until you can get back to Twin Forks and—"

"No." Gilly was with them again. "I'm afraid it's not that simple. You see, they would say Scott had an accomplice, he'd be held as an accessory to murder or unlawful flight or something." Scott could almost feel Jonah supplying the words. "Until we know who is behind this plot to frame him, we feel it best to avoid the law."

Beth cocked her head with a small frown. "Where do you come in, Miss McGill?"

"Oh, I'm just sort of second lieutenant in charge of evasive action. Not very good at it, either. The Indian is right across the street. I could see him out the rear window, hanging around the filling station over there where he can see both the front driveway and the alley."

"Oh dear!"

"I don't think you need worry, Beth," she added. "Now that he's located us, I doubt he'll follow you. You can slip out and cut across that vacant lot behind the motel, over to the next street. I'll keep watch, and if the man does go after you I'll call the police. But I'd rather not have to right now." She hated to say it. "Why don't you just head for your car and forget you ever saw us."

Beth looked troubled, still nervous. Scott could have kicked somebody—couldn't even offer to escort her, just put her in more danger. "Yeah," he said, "you pop the clutch on out of here before you catch any more of my fleas."

She had to give in. "But whenever you need me to testify you can get in touch through my mother, Miss McGill. She'll have my address as soon as I get a post office box in Chinle."

Scott sank a few more inches. The fair maiden will ride to the rescue of the ex-knight in the not-too-sharp armor, and thereby mess up her entire new career. Great, really great.

As soon as she was gone, Jonah joined them. "Damage control, not bad."

Suddenly Scott had an urge to get in that cool face. "So why don't we blow this joint before we run into a whole bunch more people whose lives I could ruin? Peel out of here fast before Geronimo can follow us—"

"I've been thinking about that," Jonah said. "I've decided to let him trail along. Maybe we can persuade him to join us for some show-and-tell, when we find a suitable spot. Right now my problem is how to cut my personnel by one-third." He focused on Gilly.

She didn't seem to notice. "Do you know what I find strange? I can hardly believe that a Navajo could be allied to a terrorist organization. It isn't in character. Their whole culture is based on harmony—a balance with nature and within themselves. They are intensely private, peaceable people."

"Any man will fight if you take his land away. Surely

you know that Congress is about to pass a bill to repossess their reservation and strip-mine it?"

"Surely, as you say, I do." Gilly gave him a look. "And the Nation may indeed present some massive resistance when the time comes. But for one of them to break away and join a gang of brutes dedicated to blowing up innocent civilians—it's difficult for me to believe."

"Not so tough if you know the whole story." Jonah seemed to make up his mind. "I can tell you this much: These cells of malcontents are recruited by a mojo man who changes his identity to suit whatever country he's in. Around the angry Sikhs he's a guru. In Central America, an Obeah doctor. In this country he calls himself 'the Shaman'—S-h-a-m-a-n—an Indian medicine man. He goes in for a lot of mystical makeup. Very few people, including his own followers, know what he looks like in the raw. I happen to be one—the guy used to buy guns from me."

Gilly sort of choked.

"It was a covert operation set up by the CIA so they could control arms sales in the Middle East. I didn't do it long. But while I was in it I met a bunch of the world's sleaziest citizens, including this scumbag, which is another reason why he'd like to eliminate me. And why the Company wants me to ID him. Of course, I doubt if he's on the scene in person. My best information puts him in South America, where he poses as a voodoo priest, face painted with wild symbols. He's been trying to overthrow every decent government they've got down there. My boys have broken up his operations in country after country."

"You got any troops on the scene here?" Scott couldn't help thinking they could use a few reinforcements.

But Jonah shook his head. "American law prohibits it, another outdated concept that must be changed if we're going to eradicate this disease. Terrorism doesn't recognize international boundaries any more than the Black Plague."

"So how does he pull off the sabotage if he isn't here?"

"Usually he picks a surrogate, some bloody-minded young guerrilla from his training camps, using whatever motivation works: money, drugs, power. He'll play on their weaknesses, teach them how to set up a cell, and recruit local help for the dirty work. I don't think he's enlisted one Indian, I think he wants to sign up the whole tribe. Supply it with stuff to make bombs, hand out some cash, they'll never dream they're helping him carry out a personal *jihad*."

"A which?"

"Holy war. He's actually a Libyan nut-case, and the deepest hatred of his heart is the Christian world, with top honors to the USA. Point is, he's basically primitive, so he'll know which strings to pull to fire up the young Navajos."

"Operation Monster Slayer." Scott recalled the words. "Sounds like some old myth."

"Well, that's probably a name the Company concocted to make the conversation ring with a deadly tone. They were feeding you words that would make you run for help, knowing the minute you mentioned 'the Shaman' I would go to red alert. I'd say they've got the date right—New Year's Eve. It's a natural, with all those crowds of people presenting big targets. What we need to do now is locate the gang's headquarters and try to find out where they've got their arsenal stockpiled."

"Their 'toys' were going to arrive at a place called 'the Shay.' "

Jonah hunched a shoulder. "Another fabrication probably."

"Or maybe not." All at once Gilly was sitting bolt-upright in her chair. "This time the CIA might be a step ahead of you." What she meant was, *she* was one-up. "For the moment I will concede that the best way to help Scott is to unearth this conspiracy. But to do it, you're going to need someone who has studied the Navajo people extensively, their ethnology, history, and culture." She said, "Mr. Pike, you are going to require my help. Believe it!"

ISABELL

□

SHE HAD always felt it to be a cheap trick, reverting to the vernacular—"Believe it!" But sometimes with a room full of tough sixteeners, it startled them into attention.

Jonah wasn't impressed. "You consider yourself an expert on Indians?"

"I studied anthropology," Isabell informed him, "specializing in the cultural history of the southwestern tribes. I did a preliminary thesis on the Navajos." And loved it. Immersed in it, she had greeted each textbook like an explorer venturing into a new cave. Until the Major had put it all in perspective. "People who retreat into the world of the dead, do it because they can't cope with the living."

Always so sure of himself—he'd have got on well with Jonah, who was having almost the same effect on her, producing those tremors of self-doubt, though his tone was entirely different. This man hardly raised his voice above a whisper.

"One question: Why are you so bent on coming along?"

Isabell searched for a credible answer, one that did not include the words "premonition" or "fear" or any reference to Scott. He was standing over by the window, looking out through the slit in the curtains with a detachment that was almost nostalgic. It was as if he were taking one last look at life. Fernando had stared that way at some invisible scenery, all through those final days, smiling at whatever she said as if it were trivial. For a moment it had lulled her fear. She'd thought he was getting his balance back—and he was. The way a man will stand at ease on the edge of a cliff in those last seconds before the big plunge.

This time she refused to be fooled. And she was bound she would not leave the boy alone out there in a cold wind which his father obviously didn't sense at all. "Mr. Pike," she said, "aside from wanting to help a friend, there are some very high stakes here in terms of human life. I can't just turn away when you obviously need me. For instance, let me ask you a question: Where do you plan to go next?"

"I intend to acquire an Indian and persuade him to be my personal guide." The casual tone underscored a ruthlessness that made her shrink inwardly.

"That might take time, even if you knew the right things to ask. For instance, would you think to inquire about the significance of Monster Slayer, and why that name could inspire a young Navajo?"

"I'm more interested in finding those explosives. You wouldn't happen to have a clue where they're stashed?"

"Maybe."

Across the room, Scott glanced over his shoulder with a curiosity that relieved his face of its inner shadows for the moment.

"Before I tell you," Isabell said, "I want your assurance that you'll let me join your effort."

Jonah made a curt gesture of consent. "Talk."

Trying to condense a whole marvelous heritage into a few words, she told them. "The Navajos are the largest Indian nation in the country and the most peaceful by nature and philosophy. But the United States government is an old, traditional enemy. It drove them off their sacred homeland once and exterminated those who resisted. Now they've got it back, they won't give it up again without a struggle. It's conceivable this time they might be persuaded to take the offensive, with some sort of guerrilla warfare, if they were approached by a leader presenting himself as a medicine man, possibly a reincarnation of one of their mythological deities. Like Monster Slayer. In Navajo legend, this was one of the Hero Twins who saved the Dineh—the People—by slaughtering the personified evils that used to walk the earth. A sort of St. George killing a variety of dragons, he represents the essence of bravery, of manhood—a very powerful concept to a young Indian. If your Shaman used this properly he might be able to inspire a band of innocent Navajos to think they were serving their deities when they do the man's dirty work." She waited for Jonah to shrug this off as unimportant.

Instead, he nodded. "That sounds like the way the guy works. Where would he choose his headquarters, do you think? The maps don't show any major population centers on the reservation."

"That's because the People are natural loners, living in family enclaves widely separated from each other. But when outside dangers threaten—and this goes back to the earliest days of the Spanish conquerors—they have historically taken refuge in one spot, a place they hold sacred because it has been soaked with their blood. It's a lovely mysterious canyon. The Navajo name for it is *Tsegi*, but the Spaniards corrupted it into Canyon de Chelly." She gave it the usual pronunciation—"d'Shay"—and finally had the brief satisfaction of startling Jonah Pike.

MOMENTS OF victory never last, she mused, when there was again time for musing. When Jonah went into action, things snapped off so fast, all she could do was obey orders and try to look cool. Jonah had directed the choreography—she and Scott moved out openly toward the truck, sending the Indian watcher off in a rush to get his own car. As soon as he was gone, Jonah had slipped out to join them, folding down into the front seat like an old tin cup, his knees under the dash, his head below eye level. Among other things, the man was a contortionist, Isabell thought, then had to hang on as Scott scorched his way out of the motel drive.

"Slow down, give him time to catch up," came the order from below.

"You mean you're still going to capture him?" Scott didn't like the idea.

"Certainly. He can tell us more about who and what and how many we're up against. Information is better than money in the bank."

So now as they drove south a red Bronco followed a mile behind. No need to stick closer—there was almost no traffic and only an occasional turnoff to a ranch.

"What I'd like to know," Isabell said at last, "is what you intend to do, exactly, after you—take him."

"Whatever's necessary." With a shrug, Jonah relegated her back to second class. "You and the boy don't have to watch."

Scott smothered a word that had the bark on it. "Why

can't you say my name? It's always 'the boy,' 'the kid.' I'm not some anonymous-type orphan, you know."

By now Jonah was back up on the seat. Sitting between them, Isabell felt an exchange of electricity that was almost tangible, as if both had batteries which had been charging over years and years.

"If you want the truth," Jonah said at last, "I have a hard time with Scott. When you were born, I'd have named you Steve."

"If you'd been around."

"Right. About then I was on the run across the Hindu Kush, taking the chase away from you as hard as I could, praying to God they'd never find out about you or your mother. That's when I knew I had to terminate the marriage. Every move I made sent out ripples that could turn into tidal waves, kicking back at you. But that doesn't mean I lost interest. I held my own private christening. Ever since, I've called you Steve."

In the herky-jerky confession Isabell detected a hint of ancient agony. But Scott was immune to overtones. He drove in stony silence, still irritated, but all over his face like headlines: What's the difference?

His father seemed oddly flustered by the silence that followed his revelation. Briskly he said, "Fact is, we may need new identities for the time being. Assume a different name and your whole persona changes. Try thinking of yourself as Steve and you'll see. It's better than a fake beard."

"I will—pick—my own—alias, thanks," Scott told him between clenched teeth.

"Whatever. But now is the time to try it on for size. Get used to it before the action begins." Jonah peered back through the camper shell at the speck of red on the road behind. He was, in fact, undergoing subtle alterations himself, Isabell realized. The emotionless face quickened with a sort of zest, reminding her of a long-ago movie where a pilot had steered a fantastic helicopter between avenues of tall buildings in a life-or-death dogfight, loving every minute of it. The man looked ten years younger than he had last night, even those hard lines had smoothed. More personas than a chameleon.

But then, she thought curiously, am I not almost as deeply changed? This woman, kiting off to save the country—who is she? Not Isabell—never that. Call me Mac! It was a private nickname she'd given herself in childhood when she was trying to toughen up and be a boy. Now, for some reason it gave her a great heart-lift, a sensation she had believed long gone. As if part of her had broken free of an invisible bondage, escaping across a harsh, magnificent wasteland of raw earth, dotted with sagebrush, studded here and there with strange shapes. Giant fins and mounds of rock had thrust upward under pressure a million years ago, turning the land savage. It could have been another planet, even, something out of a sci-fi novel: On a bright Monday morning in November of the old earth calendar Agent McGillicuddy was speeding across the moon of Jupiter on a mission where countless lives hung by a thread . . .

At least, thought Mac, it beats sophomore English class.

JONAH

❑

AMATEURS. ALWAYS an unknown. They haven't done too badly so far, but we didn't get to the sticky yet. At least they're following orders.

Setup is not bad. Handy to find a mound—the road sliced it off a hogback and left it like a huge lump, easy to drive the truck clear out of sight behind it. The Indian will have to get out of his car and come around on foot if he wants to surveille us quietly.

Steve and the woman walking away in the other direction, told 'em to make good firm tracks. Few steps and they'll be going up the far side of the mound. He'll have to follow, see what they're up to. I'll hear him as he goes past the truck.

Time to duck down under the tarp. Smells like twenty years of fish. Flatten out on the bottom, crooked, so the shape doesn't look like a man. Tarp's stiff, doesn't drape. All the Indian will see is an empty camper shell strewn with old gear.

What am I lying on? Feels like a spinner.

How long since I went fishing? Used to be pretty good with a fly rod. Maybe after all this is over, take Steve to a lake I know. Not that he'd come. Sore at me. I shouldn't have told him, shouldn't have called him Steve. Hell, what's a name? I've worn half a dozen. None ever made the papers, though. He's proud of "Scott Drummond." And why not?

Tops in his chosen game. Except that's all over now, the football malarkey. Is that what's wrong with him? Something in the eyes worries me. As if all this is a temporary annoyance compared to some bigger event. Is that why she watches him so closely?

Quite a gal. Got a hair of the bear in her. Have to concede she may turn out to be useful. . . . Stow it!

Footsteps. Breathe in millimeters, the guy may have a few natural instincts. Moves fairly well, barely brushed the back hatch when he looked in. Going on past now. Count to ten and then a . . . very . . . careful . . . scan.

Good. He's following their tracks. Dummy. No, never underestimate your opponent. He may not know the tricks, but he carries himself like a hunter.

Hidden by the jut of the mound. Move. Ease the hatch open and hope the silicone took all the squeak out. Over the tailgate, step light, he should be right around this shoulder. Thirty feet—twenty feet—*now!*

Yeah.

The guy's quick, almost dodged my chop, but "almost" doesn't count. So throw on the thumb-hitch and fasten his hands to his belt, in case he wakes up. Now, let's take a look: Driver's license, Washington, D.C., Richard Begay. Age, 35, address on K Street. No violations. Thumbprint, picture—poor likeness. Flat dark stare and a jaw like he bit down on a carpet tack. The real article looks milder. Clean-cut face, good-humor lines around the eyes. Doesn't mean a thing. Remember the fellow in Bangkok who used to crack off one-liners while he was assembling magnesium incendiaries? Nobody looks like a mad bomber.

No gun. No extra IDs. Mainly, though, no training, no tradecraft. So he can't be from the Agency or the Bureau. Which leaves the Shaman. Got to find out quick. Sun's halfway across the sky, five hours of daylight left. Come sundown you get that high-desert cold clawing its way into your gut. And two tenderfeet to provide for.

Coming back now, they looked shocked. A man is unconscious and I'm the dirty dog who did it. Written all over 'em. Even if the guy's a mass killer, it's just not nice to sucker-punch the poor fellow. The lady is chewing her lip and the kid's shoulders are ready to take on the Steelers.

Oh boy, amateurs.

SCOTT

□

WHEN IT came to bodies, which he would soon be an expert on, this one was loaded with cement. Scott grunted under the effort of moving the chunky Indian. On the opposite side, Jonah hardly seemed to notice the weight as they hauled the man over and propped him against the rocky base of the mound.

"Did you have to completely clobber him?" Scott couldn't believe. This is a terrorist?

"Only a semi-clobber. He won't even have a headache. I want his brain to function on all cylinders. But I don't want him to see me, so we'd better rig a blindfold—"

Which the Indian must have heard. His eyes popped open, black-on-black, not just reading Jonah's face—he was memorizing it. A fairly gutty thing to do, Scott thought, since he must know that Pike wasn't going to let him go back and report to the Shaman, now.

It worried Gilly, too. She stood there, tall and nose-nipped in the chilly wind. As Jonah bent over the prisoner she said, "Mr. Pike! I hope you don't intend to resort to extreme measures."

Jonah glanced around at her. "I'm going to tie his shoe-laces together so he can't get up and run. Is that okay with you?" They were city shoes like the rest of the Indian's clothes, not too hard to shed. But he wouldn't run very far in his socks, not over this stony ground. Not a bad trick, Scott had to admit. But Gilly was right—this better not get too sickening.

He said, "Why don't we leave him here and just split? By the time he gets loose we'll be long gone."

His father straightened and gave them a jerk of his head: *over there.* When they were out of hearing distance he told them once more in that low voice, "If we can find out the basics, how many people are involved in the Shaman's operation and where their base camp is, we buy time and cut our risks."

"But to use violence upon a helpless captive—" Gilly was beginning to sound like some old melodrama. Except what marred the effect, a long loop of hair had pulled loose from that knot. It waved gently out over her collar.

Jonah kept eyeing it as he said, "This isn't the place for the Geneva convention, Miss McGill. It's down-and-dirty. Your 'helpless captive' is probably a bloody-minded as-sassin. When he followed us, he invited violence."

"He hasn't attempted anything so far."

"He's been waiting for me to show up."

"Did you find a weapon when you searched him?"

"Some men don't need guns to be lethal. In this case, I'd say he's just inept. But that means it's all the more likely he's one of the terrorists. They're a bunch of fanatical volunteers with more mad enthusiasm than sense. I intend to find out exactly who he is and what he knows, if nec-

[71]

essary the hard way. But"—he held up that scarred hand—"you can try friendly persuasion first. I'll give you two exactly half an hour. Separately or together, see if you can convince him to cooperate. Meanwhile I'm going to pull his Bronco around here out of sight and toss it. There may be some clue that will help."

A half an hour. About the time it takes to play one quarter with a few time-outs. Except the man over there had used up his options. Scott hunched over, hands on knees in his huddle stance—always seemed to think better that way. And what he wondered was, how do you tell a lady her hair is sprouting? The damned Indian was going to die of hysterics, which maybe is the easy way to go. He felt a sickly chuckle trying to come up.

"Any ideas?" Gilly had joined the huddle.

Scott said, "Yeah. Why don't I try to scare this yoyo with some tough talk? Then you be good guy, step in and butter him up. Only you might want . . . to change . . . your image."

She looked down at herself. "I don't see how—" And then her hand discovered the loose topknot. "Oh. Thanks. Next time, come right on out and tell me the worst."

A pretty classy old girl. How do you get that mature? *I'll never know.* The odd twist of thought brought a kind of relief. From where he sat right now, the world was looking fairly cruddy. And it was going to get worse in a minute, if he couldn't con this Navajo into talking. Never was great on gory movies, even where you knew it wasn't real blood. This was a hundred percent live coverage. So give it a shot.

As he strolled toward the man, the swarthy face could have been carved of juniper wood. Black hair scattered across the broad forehead, dark eyes flat as ink. Tough body, built a little odd—torso like a tackle with running-back hips—but plenty muscular and tight with resistance. Scott slouched on up to stand over him—at least Indiana Jones had a whip over his shoulder he could kind of toy with.

Taking a long breath, he said, "So. I guess you know who I am, you've been following me all over the world. You want to tell me why? Why you'd want to bug a nice girl like Beth Frawley? Man, you got her terrified, you ever think of that?"

No reaction.

Scott tried again. "For your information, that girl has nothing to do with anything. I never met her before the football game. Is that where you picked us up? Right after you killed the FBI man, maybe that's when you were tucking him away in the trunk of my car? Look, we know you're not with the law, or you'd have arrested me by now. You couldn't be CIA, they wouldn't let you empty their trash. So that makes you a Monster Slayer. Am I getting warm? How's the old Shaman these days?"

Not a flicker, the Indian's face was super-blank.

"We know he's trying to locate us and put the screws to Jonah. By the way, speaking of screws, you're about to get a demonstration from an expert. Why not save yourself some blood and teeth and toenails and talk to me?"

The man's look shifted a fraction as Gilly came over to join them, holding a plastic cup that steamed slightly in the afternoon air. Crouching at the Indian's side, she said, "I thought you could use some hot coffee—well, actually it isn't too hot. It's been in the thermos ever since this morning."

Scott put on a scowl and stood up. "You don't have to be so nice to a guy who murders women and children for kicks. I mean, for corn-sake, Miss McGill!" And stalked off a short distance. With his back turned he could only catch an occasional word as she spoke softly.

" . . . can't really believe you would . . . always thought the Navajo people . . . know that they live for beauty, harmony . . . see you hurt, but unless you . . . *Please*, Mr. Begay."

The Indian wasn't buying. And now Jonah came toward them carrying a small Craftsman toolbox, about the size to hold a power drill. As he joined them he said, "We have the answer to one question. I found this under the driver's seat in the Bronco." Flipping the latch, he opened the lid—inside were three red cylinders wound together with wire and attached to a round instrument with a dial face. "It's not armed. See that loose wire? That has to be connected to the timer; then all you do is set the thing running and when it explodes, you are long gone. Nice work, incidentally." He waved the box in a sort of salute to the prisoner.

The Navajo's hardpan had cracked wide open. "Under the . . ." he licked his lips. "Under the driver's seat?"

Jonah laughed—that was some deadly laugh. "Don't tell me: You never saw it before."

The Indian shook his head. "I wouldn't know how to make a—whatever it is—not if my life depended on it."

"How about your death?" Jonah handed the bomb to Gilly. "You two take a walk."

"Wait!" She was staring half-hypnotized by the ugly thing. "There could be another explanation. This loose wire—suppose the bomb was meant for Mr. Begay? And the wire came loose, which is why it didn't go off as intended?"

"That's gotta be it." The Indian's face was slick with a film of sweat as he shivered in the deepening chill. "Look,

I'm not one of these terrorists you're talking about. I don't even know who they are."

"Sure, that's why you've been on our trail like a bluetick hound."

"I swear! The people who planted that thing must be the same ones who killed agent Holdrege."

"Convince me." Jonah hung there, grimly.

From the west, long shadows stretched toward them now. The Navajo looked away toward the mountains as if he were seeing ghosts—of Geronimo and Sitting Bull and Chief Joseph—images that made him wince as he said, "I'm with the FBI."

A G-man?

"He's got to be kidding." Scott looked at his father and saw the same doubts. Even Gilly was skeptical.

"Where's your ID?" Jonah demanded.

The Navajo looked embarrassed. "I mailed my credentials to myself at Chinle. I figured if I needed them, I could pick them up at the post office. I wouldn't want to walk around carrying them down there. My people don't know I work for the Bureau."

"Why Chinle?"

"Well—I mean when you took the road south, you had to be heading there. Where else?"

"You're lying. As fast as you followed us, you didn't have time to mail anything. You're a bungler and a fool and the Bureau wouldn't even give you a door pass."

The brown face turned a shade of burnt red. "Okay, so I never got much field training, just a few weeks of basic. I went into the Bureau straight out of Harvard Law School. When the recruiter came up there last year he fed me a sales pitch, how I could help my people out. Then they stick me at a desk doing paperwork for drug cases down in Miami. All they wanted was a token savage on the payroll. Until they ran into trouble on the Reservation. Then they send me out here as advisor to Holdrege, except he didn't want any advice. He tells me to tail the boy and see if an older man tries to make contact. Says the CIA wants the guy—do not approach. If I see him, I call the experts. Next I know, Holdrege vanishes. When I check in at his office, I find it's been turned upside-down. I guess he walked in at the wrong minute—I found some blood-stains. So I call the home office—they say continue to watch the kid. But by the time I get back to his house there's cop cars crawling all over and the word is, the boy killed somebody."

Scott shook his head. "It had to be the Shaman's gang. They must have figured I left an address with Holdrege where they could locate Jonah. Then they set up the frame on me. And you believed it?"

"Of course not. I was on your tail all that afternoon. I went to the police station and flashed my badge at the Chief. Told him I could alibi you. But he says maybe you had an accomplice, which I couldn't argue with—I'm thinking about this unknown man I'm not supposed to approach. So I heard them say the kid is headed for Utah— I go to Utah. Lucked onto him next morning, lost him, then I noticed that girl. They were talking at the game, I thought maybe she's part of the plot. At least she led me to the motel. So I took up the tail again until a ton of brick falls on me."

"It would have saved time if you'd told us this in the beginning," Jonah said.

"How could I?" With a touch of anger. "You're ob-viously this wanted man. Probably the killer, I don't know. It's all somehow tied up to trouble down in the Nation, maybe you're the instigator of that. After you knocked me out, I guess I had a few doubts, whether I should trust you."

Jonah stared off into space for a long minute. Then, "The story is so crazy, I'm inclined to believe it. Who could make all that up?" He shook his head and went over to jerk the knot loose, freeing the man's hands, letting him tie his own shoes with fingers that didn't work too well.

Gilly drew a long breath of relief. "Is there any kind of stove in the camper where I could heat this coffee?"

"Coleman two-burner. At the bottom of that box of fishing stuff."

Tucking the bomb under her arm, she headed for the pickup. Scott wanted to go along, just to make sure she didn't drop the thing. But Jonah was still burning questions at the Indian.

"I don't know," Begay kept saying. "I don't know anything. I don't even know who I am or what I am. The reason I mailed my ID last night, I thought maybe I'd quit this damned job. The government doesn't give me any details or explanation. It's as if they think I haven't got the brain for it, that I don't need to know what's going on with my own people. The Dineh—they're the ones getting the short end of the stick, no matter what goes down, count on it. I should be with them."

"Even if they resort to anarchy?"

The Indian returned Jonah's stare. "One man's guerrilla is another man's freedom fighter. You ever have your home foreclosed? Some stranger come along, say 'Hit the bricks, fella, you don't live here any more'?"

"I'm not talking about self-defense. I'm asking you if a clever international crook could use the current situation to enlist your kinfolk in a wide-scale bloodbath? Would they be willing to set off bombs for him all across the country while he slips away back to the Middle East, leaving them to take the heat?"

Begay looked confused. "What's this got to do with the Middle East?"

"Good question." Jonah turned to head for the truck. "You'll get your answer the hard way if you join the Shaman's gang."

"Wait a minute." The Indian followed him. "I never heard of this Shaman. We seldom call our holy men that. And a genuine *haatalii* wouldn't touch a bomb. If this phony is conning the Navajo, I want to know about it."

At the truck, Gilly handed them cups full of coffee that steamed. "Maybe we could all work together, Mr. Pike," she said. "We are about to go into a foreign settlement—down there on the Reservation we'll stand out like white mice in a woodpile. We really need Richard." Then she caught some expression on the Navajo's face and said, "I'm sorry. I didn't mean to get familiar. It's the schoolteacher in me."

Begay grinned at her suddenly, a flash of white teeth that were startling in the brown of his face. "It was a schoolmarm who hung that name on me long ago. Really nice white lady, she figured it would look more civilized on the roll call than 'Nighthawk.' " Then he added dryly, "As a symbol, the nighthawk isn't much of a killer, eats mostly insects. But it has a few moves that aren't too shabby."

MOVES. *I'm the guy who used to have them.* Scott drove the pickup with a heavy foot, ramming it over the rough unmended highway. I must have lost my edge completely.

[78]

Had to go and open my big mouth: "Shouldn't we maybe dispose of the bomb, bury it or something?"

I'll bet the old man had a big laugh out of that, behind his poker face. But how would I know it was a fake? Made up of fuses and copper wire and the dial off an old ammeter—"Charge" and "Discharge"—anybody could figure it, even a woman, for corn-sake. Of course Gilly had held the thing in her hands. And it took a heads-up play to join in the scam and feed Jonah the exactly right question: "Suppose the bomb was meant for Mr. Begay?" Popped the lid off the Indian like a can opener.

Even Jonah had been impressed. After the tailgate party broke up and they were back on the road, he'd said, "Miss McGill, we owe you one. If you hadn't played shill, our Navajo might never have taken the bait. He was too stunned to figure it out for himself."

She looked pleased. "I'm just curious—how did you put that thing together so fast?"

"Junk from the back of the truck—flares, battery tester, tools, wire."

My father, the genius.

Scott couldn't even explain the stew of angers, old and new, that simmered in him as they drove in silence through the night.

Darkness had come swiftly and completely. Cold, too. The stars looked frozen solid into the icy sheet of the sky as if they'd died and quit beaming down light, leaving the world in inky shadow. Empty land, deserted except for the two vehicles. Far ahead a pair of red taillights looked like twin insects dancing in the dark. The Indian's Bronco was taking the bumps like a horse heading home.

"I don't get it," Scott muttered, then wished he'd kept

shut. If your brain is numb, why advertise it? But his father was looking across, waiting for the rest of the question. "Well, I mean, why is this guy suddenly our best friend? How do you know we can trust him?"

"We have to bunk down somewhere for the night," Jonah said, "and there are obviously no motels handy. Seems to me a piece of luck that he asked us to stay at his place. Gives us temporary cover, and we may be able to use him to get information from his brothers that we couldn't come by. And for the record," he added, "I don't trust anybody but myself."

"Thanks for sharing that." Scott saw a pothole notching his left headlight and steered straight at it. Crump! As he felt the others stare at him, he kicked the accelerator harder, the truck rattling in all its joints as they tore through the night.

My father, Mr. Wonderful.

NIGHTHAWK

☐

HOME. THE old tongue had no better word for this feeling of belong-to-the-place-forever. No matter how many years slipped by, on a campus, in an apartment, an office—this was home. Even by dark, Nighthawk recognized Dinetah. He wasn't sure that it recognized him.

Not the same Navajo boy who had climbed on the bus. He'd been nineteen then, green. Another handy Americanism for the years when you are soft-to-the-sun-of-midday. He had been green as a new sapling, but the scorching competition of a big university had toughened him. The cynical world of Washington, D.C., had dried up a lot of juices. He had to wonder what was left of the root.

Out under the night sky the sacred land lay mysterious, as awesome as he remembered. The cold night air felt good in his nostrils. To be alone—well, not quite. Nighthawk glanced in his rearview mirror where the hard-eyed headlights followed in the distance.

Tough man, that Jonah Pike. The look of a hunting bird

that kills with no feeling. Well, there have to be predators, but he wished he could be rid of this one. That's why he'd decided to let them stay at the shack. Settle them where he could find them again and then get to town, search out members of the family, try to learn the truth about what was going on.

Terrorism. No one had to explain that word to a Navajo. There had been times lately when he had laughed inside to hear the neat men in his office discuss the horrors of the Middle East in such fastidious righteousness, deploring the genocide, shocked over the killing of innocent civilians. Not one of them ever heard of Fort Sumner. They wouldn't have believed their white man's hero, Kit Carson, ever marched a starving hoard of men, women, and children to a concentration camp for no reason except that they were Indian and they stood in the way of the prospectors who dreamed gold might exist in the earth of Dinetah. Thank the deities, there was none.

And so the Nation, what was left of it, was allowed to come back. They'd survived and multiplied, in spite of cold and heat and drought that left no grazing for the sheep. In spite of government interference, giving large chunks of the sacred land to the Hopi and Apache. To see it all threatened now by some act of Congress? No, they wouldn't roll over and submit, not this time.

When the bill had been proposed Nighthawk couldn't believe it would get out of committee. But it did. It was coming to a vote soon. And all the white men would need was to have an excuse—a bunch of Navajos blowing stuff up, they've exterminated whole tribes for less.

This "Shaman" story sounded like some crazy spy novel. And yet she was taking it seriously, the woman, and she was no fool. Fine-looking lady, with the kind of quiet intelligence you seldom see along with so much warmth. She was worried, and something else—an air of captivity about her, a tenseness. Could she be a prisoner, she and the boy? He seemed to be in a kind of insurrection too. Is the man forcing them to go along with him, this character with the stone eyes? Pretty hard fist, too—Nighthawk's neck still throbbed.

Need the old medicine bag. For the first time in years he thought of it—his grandfather's pouch with its holy contents. He had left it with a cousin when he went east— what they would have said at Harvard if you carried a sack of herbs around in your loincloth. But now he'd like to hold again the piece of turquoise, to try to remember a few ancient words, to grope his way back toward beauty. If he could?

Can I go back? Or is it too late? Will all that polish on my shoes make my feet heavy? Has the white man's haircut let all the good Navajo thoughts escape forever? Do I really want to be an Indian again?

There was much to be considered.

ISABELL

❑

A STRANGE small fantasy seized her, born of the oddness of these last days. Relieved of the numbing reality of her life, Isabell played make-believe.

She glimpsed herself as a Navajo woman. All the more vivid because it had to be fleeting, she felt herself to be young again, bronze-skinned, black of hair. *My name is Drifting Wood.* (Do the Dineh give their girl children war names, like the boys?)

You know so little, how dare you try to improvise? Her stern classroom ethic took over again. She roused to the ruthless cold of the small outhouse. Buttoning the wool coat with numb fingers, she dismissed her imaginings. *Just call me Blue Buns.* With a touch of self-contempt, she stepped out into the wintry morning sunlight—and was captivated all over again. The vast gray ocean of the high desert surged so majestically into the distance to wash against the far-flung mesas, she wanted desperately to claim it for her own. Just a private compact, no one need know.

To honor the four sacred mountains, was that so wrong? What more impressive, magnificent symbol of an Almighty? She wished she were the child of Changing Woman, the universal mother-figure robed in turquoise. And if White Shell Girl had taken her by the hand and led her through the *Kinaalda* ritual, Isabell wondered if she might not have taken charge of her own life while it was still young. Surely an ancient ceremony would be a better rite of passage than, say, the winning of the Triple A title?

As she headed for the shack, she settled into a familiar worry pattern. Scott had spent a restless night—she knew, because they had shared the only bed. Wrapped in separate blankets that Nighthawk had provided, before he went off to town, they had both done some tossing and turning. But at least they had been inside. Jonah had slept in the truck, which he had pulled up close behind the building.

Nighthawk's ancestral home was a two-room shanty that had once been red, to judge by the shreds of paint that still clung to the weathered boards. As she mounted the back steps and went in, she found Pike pumping the antiquated Coleman stove, but his eyes were focused on the boy. Scott stood across the room, hefting a length of firewood with that rebellious look that he'd worn ever since they'd left Moab.

For his part, Jonah was obviously getting tired of explaining. "Don't you get it? If there's nobody here, how would it look to have smoke come from the chimney? Come on, that play of yours, the one they call the 'Gamebuster,' it depends on deception, doesn't it?"

Disconcerted, the boy threw the log back into the woodbox by the door. "So what's *your* game plan? What do we do when the Indian comes back with a war party of his friends? Do you have a gun, even?"

Jonah shook his head, a slight gesture of impatience. "We keep an eye out and when our host shows up, we decide what to do. Over those ruts it will take him five minutes to get to the shack, plenty of time to chart a course of action."

"Unless he comes from the rear. Indians ride horses, you know." Scott headed for the back door.

"Don't go out there. You can stand watch just as well inside."

"Listen, there's only two people I take orders from, my coach and my *dad*." Scott slammed the door behind him.

Isabell bit back a few words she was tempted to let fly. As she watched the boy tramp off toward the jumble of rickety corrals behind the shack, she just hoped that temper was a good sign. Before Jonah could follow, she intercepted him.

"If you're wise, you'll come down off your high horse and treat him like one of the team. Let him explore," she advised. "There's an old hogan back there." The primitive eight-sided hut had its roof caved in, the doorway blocked by a piece of warped plywood. "Why don't you stand lookout up front? I'll take over the cooking chores." When she felt the coffeepot, it was hardly lukewarm, and the pan of sliced Spam hadn't even begun to sizzle.

As Jonah took up position at the front window, he said abruptly, "You know the kid better than I do. What's eating him?"

She hadn't expected the question. "Aside from being accused of murder and so forth?"

"I didn't frame him. Why's he so hostile?"

"You also haven't exactly been around in times of crisis, up to now. You didn't really expect him to accept you automatically on first meeting?"

"As a parent, no. But you'd think he would recognize that right now I'm the authority on survival. Not that he cares about that. From the way he was driving last night you'd think he had a death wish."

Isabell shuddered in spite of herself. What would he do if she spilled the truth? He'd be skeptical, she was sure. Suicide would seem utterly alien to a man like Jonah Pike, especially if the cause were the loss of a sports career. And yet she was tempted to tell him anyway—he had a right to know. It might even rattle that cocksureness.

Then, before she could make up her mind, Scott was coming back, feet clumping on the back stoop. He looked better—cheeks ruddy, the light hair blown askew. "Hey, maybe I found it—out back, there's a kind of bunker where they must have stored their dynamite. Or something valuable, anyway, because somebody punched a hole in the wall and cleaned the place out."

Isabell hated to deflate him. "That hut is the original family dwelling. When a person dies inside a hogan, they knock a hole in the wall so the spirit can escape."

Scott looked disappointed. Picking up a slice of bread he folded it around two large pieces of undercooked Spam. "So why can't the dead guy's ghost just ankle on out the front?"

"I'm not sure. They always nail boards over the door so no one can inadvertently enter. The Navajo believe that death is the greatest of all evils, the worst curse that can fall on a house. The place is considered tainted forever."

Scott stared at his sandwich. "What do a bunch of Indians know, anyway? The Vikings thought it was neat to go out in style, put the guy in his own boat and set it afire. That's what I call class."

And again recognition gripped her. Fernando had bought

[87]

himself a complete outfit of black leather, a silver-plated chain and, for some reason, one white spangled glove.

She was jarred out of her dreadful introspection by a smothered sound of frustration. Jonah at the window. "I don't like it, all this waiting. Smells like a double cross." But a moment later he came to attention. "There he is. Turning in at the road." And after a few seconds, he added, "Alone."

In faded denims and a scruffy Stetson, the Indian seemed closer to his heritage—he looked like any Navajo bringing home some groceries. Heaving out the two large paper bags, he headed for the shack. But the body language was expressive, at least to Isabell. Stiff neck, dogged steps. He didn't want to come back here. He doesn't trust Jonah, and why should he? It must have been a temptation to lose himself among his own people. Instead, he brings us supplies. A man of conscience.

Scott had the door open, grabbing the shopping sacks, rummaging, seizing. He snatched out a carton of eggs and brought it to Isabell like an offering to the Earth Mother.

"Well, what's the word?" Jonah was demanding of the Indian.

"Lots of 'em. Whole lotta words." His black eyes hidden by a quizzical squint, Nighthawk looked more sure of himself. There was an indefinable difference in his speech. To Gilly he said, "If you've volunteered to cook, you'll find a big frying pan in that cupboard. We could all use some breakfast, I reckon." He went to start a fire in the stove.

"I believe we should keep a low profile." Jonah let exasperation color his tone.

"Whole Nation knows I'm home. Look odd if there wasn't some smoke," the Indian told him. "By the way, I mentioned to my cousin that I was entertaining some friends from back east. Meteorologists, came down here to study the weather patterns. It seemed like a safe cover. Anybody asks, all you've got to do is make up some bunk about the jet stream."

Jonah smothered a snort of disgust. "The Shaman's gang isn't going to be fooled by that. The minute they hear there are strangers—"

"Shaman," mused Nighthawk. "Now that's one of those words that's going around town. But from what I gather, nobody has ever seen this guy. Supposed to be a medicine man. Or a witch—that's what the People are wondering. On the other hand, if he's anti-USA they're willing to give him the benefit of the doubt."

As Isabell got the fire going, the smell of bacon and woodsmoke began to fill the room. Scott hovered off her left elbow, plate in hand. Over his shoulder he asked Nighthawk, "If they haven't met him in person, how does he get them to sign up?"

"Good question." The Navajo nodded. "Every time I asked it, folks didn't hear me. I'm not their favorite son. When I went back east to school, I told them I was going to find legal ways out of our tribal problems. Now they wonder what I ever did for them, namely, nothing. So I can't expect them to include me in their important councils."

"Four, please, or maybe five—" Scott was watching her break eggs into the pan. "Over easy."

Jonah was scowling as if food were a device of the devil to tempt people into sin. He headed for the back door. "I'm going to take a scout around."

By the kitchen window, Nighthawk watched him go, then turned to Isabell. "Are you okay?"

The question surprised her. "I'm fine, thanks to that warm blanket you gave me. It's a beautiful thing."

"My grandmother was a great weaver. She'd be pleased that you rested well under it."

What a marvelous smile, she thought, as she set plates on the table and went back for the coffee. It brought a ridiculous surge of happiness—Mac, dishing up grub to her gang (while somewhere to the northeast, the eleven o'clock comp class tore each other limb from limb and a substitute teacher self-destructed).

Scott was digging into his food, but Nighthawk had settled for coffee, obviously building up to something. Abruptly he said, "The real reason I came back here, I wondered if you two want to go on with all this. I can alibi the boy, I'm FBI, the local law in Twin Forks will have to listen to me. I could give you a lift back home and leave Superman out there to fight his own battles."

"No!" Isabell was shocked at how fast she rejected the suggestion. As if she couldn't bear to retreat now, leaving an important moment of her life unfinished, losing the bonds that held her to Scott. Flushing a little, she said, "It's not quite that simple. You see, Mr. Pike is afraid these terrorists might kidnap his son and hold Scott hostage."

"You're that man's *son?*" The Indian's cup clattered in the saucer.

Scott nodded. "Technically."

"What does that mean?"

"He cut out on us—my mom and me—when I was born."

"To save his family from becoming endangered by his peculiar profession. He's led his whole life as an undercover agent—he didn't want to see them drawn in." Isabell had to say it in all fairness.

"I never met him until two days ago," the boy added with visible bitterness.

[90]

"After he had flown halfway across the world at a phone call." Isabell turned to Nighthawk. "All this is very complex and I don't think we can walk away from it, even if we wanted to."

Then Jonah was back. "If you're sufficiently fed, maybe you can answer a few more questions?"

Deliberately Nighthawk refilled his cup. "Maybe."

Angling his long powerful body against the window frame, still keeping an eye out toward the road, Jonah asked, "What's your reading of the mood among your people?"

"The old-timers are cautious. They want to see this mystic in person before they decide whether his medicine is good. On the other hand, Uncle Sam keeps bringing in more troops every day. They're camped just south of here. And the motel in Chinle is full of engineers, mining officials, construction workers. They're setting up offices, putting up prefab warehouses. There's a lot of resentment growing, especially among the Navajo boys, they've got the itch to fight. Many of them have come from the cities, Albuquerque, Phoenix, where they went to try to scratch out a living. They've grown away from the old traditions of peace and balance, to walk in beauty and all that. They just know that this land is all the birthright they've got. They're caught between cultures—I know how they feel. When you look in the mirror and you don't see anybody, you've got to turn into somebody, even if it's a warrior. You need that self-respect. It's all an Indian's got going for him."

Scott looked up, his face an open book of utter comprehension.

Jonah was unconvinced. "But would they be willing to die?"

The boy said, "Damned straight they would."

His father glanced at him, puzzled. Then around at the rest of his crew, as if he wished for better. "These young militants—how many? Best guess?"

Nighthawk's broad shoulders rose and fell. "From what I hear by moccasin telegraph, around the laundromat and post office, there's a bunch hiding out in the woods above the Canyon, kind of waiting for a sign or an omen. How many? I don't know, maybe a thousand or two." The brown face broke into one of those swift grins. "You look like that guy in the shark movie, when he says, 'We're gonna need a bigger boat.' "

"I don't understand," Isabell said. "I thought they would be down in the Canyon, in the caves."

"We learned a few things from Kit Carson." The Navajo spoke the name like an obscenity. "This time they stay on top, in camps back in the cedars. Nobody can bottle them up. The only folks down in the bottoms are the rock-busters, some kind of archaeological dig."

Scott jerked to attention. "I forgot about that!"

"It's odd, come to think." Nighthawk shook his head. "Strange that the tribal council would let a crew of out-siders in there at a time like this. Especially where their camp is, in a narrow branch off the main arm of Canyon del Muerto. A lot of bloody history there. You don't reckon that could be the Shaman's gang?"

"It's the kind of cover he uses!" Jonah's face had quick-ened as he listened. "It's his MO, all right, to set up a phony front and establish a cadre of his recruiters under some pseudo-legitimate disguise. There's probably one gen-uine Navajo to act as liaison with the locals."

"Big Cat. I kept hearing that name. He's the one in charge of this dig, but when I asked what his family is—if you're Dineh, you got to have a family tree—nobody seemed to know. They didn't want to talk about it, come to think."

Scott was on his feet. "Beth Frawley."

Jonah eyed him. "What about her?"

"She was on her way there. It's her first job—she was all excited. My Lord, she's going to walk into a wasp's nest." He kicked his chair aside. "I've got to stop her."

"Wait a minute. Let's think about this."

"No time. Maybe I can get to her before she checks in. She said she was planning a side trip. If I can get to that post office before she does, I can intercept her when she goes to rent a box." He was struggling into his Mackinaw.

Jonah moved to stand between him and the door. "You're going nowhere. Give me those—" He made a quick move for the keys that already dangled from Scott's fingers.

"In your face!" The boy made it look easy—the side step, the hip-jolt, and Jonah was down. As the door slammed, Nighthawk moved to help the man on the floor. Isabell was still sitting stunned when the truck roared to life, kicking gravel as it spun away.

JONAH

❏

GREAT MOVES . . . could train that kid . . .

Sit up? Hooo-boy, not yet. What'd I hit? The wood hopper, as I went down. All happened so fast.

Somebody's yelling . . . "You've got to go after him, Nighthawk!"

No. Say it out loud: "No."

Argument going on, what's she saying? " . . . give me the keys."

Try again. "No!" Came out better that time, got their attention. "Need the Bronco here . . . got to have wheels." If the room would quit spinning. "Wait a few minutes, we'll all go."

"But we may never catch him! We mustn't let him get away from us, you don't understand."

Lady, don't explain anything right now. A demolition crew is tearing down my skull, brick by brick, and I am seeing double—two Indians taking off their pants. No, he's going for a money belt. Sack. Like the Kurds wear, leather pouch for valuables. Taking out packet . . .

She's pouring coffee, okay, good stimulant. But what's he up to, adding powder from that packet?

She asks it. "What's that you're putting into his cup?"

"No idea." Indian's a funny man. "This is my grandfather's medicine bag. I don't know exactly what this stuff is, some sort of ground-up root. But I know it clears your head."

Search Navajo face, trickery? No. Go on, drink, you have to trust. Tastes like raw cinnamon, but it's taking hold. Better than whiskey, numbs the nerve ends like a local anesthetic. The jackhammer's still going, but it's over on the next block. Whatever that junk is, he ought to patent it.

"Does it help?"

"Yep." Let's try again, sit up. Not bad.

The lady hovers, her eyes bright with worry, but not for me. "I hate to rush you, but there's something you should know about Scott. Two weeks ago he suffered an injury on the football field—"

"I had a copy of the X-rays the day after it happened." What does she think, I don't keep an eye on my son? "I had my own experts look at them. They seem to think the problem of future disability is not all that likely. His doctor probably exaggerated, to get him out of a dangerous sport. Just as well. The boy can stop playing games and get serious with his life."

She's shocked. "Well, that's not the way Scott sees it. All he can think is how everything he ever planned or cared about has been wrecked. He's lost the world, and when you're eighteen it can seem utterly permanent. I've seen it happen. He doesn't care whether he lives or dies. He's going off into danger like a kamikaze. Now do you understand why we've got to follow him? At once?"

She's got to be kidding. And yet the kid does have a look, as if we're all only footnotes to a bigger scenario. No, it's exactly as serious as she thinks it is. She knows him, you don't. Learn to learn.

Nighthawk's trying to calm her down. "The boy will be okay as long as he's hunting for the girl. Let's hope he doesn't find her too soon—not until we catch up with him." He's looking at me, telegraphing something he doesn't want to say out loud.

And all at once it comes deadly clear. Obvious. On your feet, buddy, it's a lot later than you thought!

SCOTT

□

GRINNING OUT loud, Scott smacked the wheel so hard his hand stung. Man, it felt great to throw that body check! Mister Big Shot, ordering everybody around—shouldn't have tried to grab those keys. Tough Tillie.

He felt light, free, the way you do when you're on your game. With fingertip control, he steered the pickup smoothly over the uneven road. Back in charge of his own life, for however long he decided to hang onto it. Glancing in his rearview mirror, he half-expected to see a red Bronco back there on his tail, but the highway was empty.

Maybe I had no right to help myself to his truck, but Jonah would never have wanted to waste time going after some unknown girl. And that's the difference. Me, I just happen to care about women, any kind of woman, they need help.

Even Gilly, for all she acts like Lady MacBeth in class, get her out here in the real world and she's nervous as a cat. Fidgeting with those fake glasses—on again, off again—could be she's having trouble with her own image? That mirror Nighthawk mentioned? Now there's a guy who got his face back fast. Put on some old jeans, a crummy hat, and desert boots, and he's a full-time Navajo. For me, I guess what would do it is Clint. He'd take one look at me and I'm Number Eight again.

Scott went out of focus, his eyes turned inward, back to a hot day. Out of the roar of the grandstands came one deep bellow of joy as the receiver pulled the ball down and took it into the end zone. There in the front row at the fifty-yard line, Clint was walloping everybody on the back, his big face split wide open with pride. *Lord, I wish he was here.*

No, I'm glad he isn't. Scott had to admit, down in the oil fields Clint was all-pro. But he'd be lost in a dirty mess like this. He never cared for real violence, he wouldn't even look at the news when it got bloody. He wouldn't personally think of going after a bunch of terrorists, he'd call in the army. He'd sure as hell never get himself up as a ragged old bum. . . .

Scott checked the mirror again. The blacktop was empty for about 1,000 miles behind him. On all sides the long reaches of the land looked deserted. And then his eye snagged on a thin thread of white—smoke rising from a hogan. He began to pick out others, gray on gray, tucked into the folds of the ancient earth. People were actually living in all that nowhere. Probably watching an out-of-state pickup busting down the highway. Alone.

Which was great. A relief to be rid of the old man. "Don't do that!" "You're not going anywhere!" Never thought he could be taken down. Of course, he wasn't expecting an attack from his own team.

Corn-sake, I didn't really hurt the guy? I didn't hit him

that hard. Na-a-a, you could drop a linebacker on Jonah, he wouldn't feel it. Unless he bumped his head when he fell, come to think, there was a kind of "clunk."

Don't sweat it. Gilly will pick up his pieces, she's into repairing busted people.

And Nighthawk would know what to do. Scott felt an odd respect for the Indian. For all he acted nervous and a little dumb, still you sensed a whole other person beneath the surface, a man you wouldn't mind having along in a pinch.

Which it might come to. Face it, the whole terrorist lineup was probably hiding out in this Canyon de Chelly. Which ought to be around here fairly close-by. Scott searched the scenery to either side of the highway, but so far no sign of a rift. Canyon could be a drop-off type, like the Royal Gorge, where you don't see it until you practically fall into it.

Maybe once I tip off Beth, make sure she doesn't get herself in trouble, I may just scout the enemy's territory. Show the old man I'm not a complete idiot.

And that was what it really was about—in a flash of inner truth, Scott conceded. From the minute he'd heard that unemotional voice on the phone he had waited for a sign, any sort of recognition, a small spark of personal warmth, father-to-son. Not that Jonah was the sort to go around slapping people on the back: You are one great kid, my long-lost boy. Nothing like that. But it wouldn't break his face to smile once or twice, maybe nod, like *nice going.*

So forget it. You're not a kid anymore, to have day dreams. Scott used to make them up—notions about what it would be like. When he was little, it was always a birthday party and this stranger would show up at the door with a great present. Later, he pictured it happening after a big game. Some guy would step down out of the stands— "Good win, son"—disappear into the night. He could never quite visualize the face, but he knew he'd know him, there would be a bond . . .

Crazy. Why should he give you a thought, he's had his own problems, with Turkish prisons and escapes and gun-running, and all that—you don't stop to moon around over some kid you never saw. And when you do meet him, what's to like? I haven't exactly shown him my best stuff.

Scott tried to keep his eyes off the rearview mirror. Okay, so it was a cheap shot. I'm sorry. I will go back and apologize, as soon as I find the girl.

Ahead, he saw a scatter of buildings, must be the town of Chinle. Not much town—it made Twin Forks look big. A straggle of houses off to the left, a few boxy apartment-type buildings such as the government might put up. Along the road he was passing a string of gas storage tanks, corrals, acres of parked earthmovers—real big wheels, the kind that can chew up scenery fast. And there on the left a sign that pointed east: *To Canyon de Chelly*—3 miles.

In the pit of his belly he felt a small kernel of heat like a burning peanut. He knew the sensation, it came when you were going into a tough game against some down-and-dirty team. It meant your pilot light was lit. Take the field.

As he started to swing into the turn, he put on brake. Directly opposite the intersection was a shopping center, not very big. Restaurant, dry cleaners, clothing store, ice cream shop, and some Stars and Stripes.

What do you bet the only place on the Reservation where they fly Old Glory is the U.S. post office?

Putting the wheel over, Scott swerved into the parking

lot, taking the first open slot. And found himself beside a familiar butter-colored Toyota. Cutting the engine, he slumped low in the seat. But the man in the next car didn't even glance his way. Half-hidden behind a map, cute little fedora down over his eyes—it was Buford all right. He was staking out the place, it was written all over him; watching for somebody.

Probably me! And if he spots me, it's all going to get very complicated. Scott moved to the far side of the seat. When a goof-off gang of hard hats came strolling past, he eased out and mingled. They were heading for a convenience shop that looked brand-new, decorated el cheap-o, lots of formica and displays of Timex watches, Bic lighters, racks of Twinkies. I'll bet Nighthawk never ate a Twinkie in his life. Half-hidden behind the magazine rack, Scott could see out the big front window. Beginning to get the picture: Buford wrangling dinner at their house, asking all those questions. "When will your dad be home?" He's one of them, all right. Taking advantage of Mom that way, I could kill the—

Suddenly the pudgy little man had put the map aside and was getting out of the car, moving lightly, stalking—who? Scott searched around and got a jolt. Beth Frawley had just come out of the post office, her pink stocking cap perking along as she walked briskly. Buford took up the tail thirty yards behind her, his dark overcoat had "sneaky" written in every wrinkle.

He must have seen her come to our room at the motel. Now he thinks he'll pump her for information. I've got to get to her first, only how? I could probably take him in a normal fight, but who knows what sort of piece he's carrying?

Once more Scott glanced along the back road, but he

wasn't really expecting to see any troops. All he could do was follow the lead and play it by ear. When he rounded the end of the shopping center, he saw Beth heading for a building that looked brand-new. Prefab, it still had the government packing labels on the units which had been whacked together to make a boxy warehouse. Beth walked straight on in; Buford eased up, then he was inside too.

As Scott came up to the door, he saw a row of small signs tacked beside it. One of them read:

MUSEUM EXPEDITIONS
OFFICE

So—you do what you have to. He turned the handle and let himself into the building.

A narrow hallway stretched the length of it, closed doors had names on them, engineering firms, contractors. At the far end, Buford was trying the knob of one—he peered in and straightened.

"Well, well." Out of nowhere there was a gun in his plump fist. "Hello, sweet-cakes. Nice place you've got. Just the spot for a chat."

When the play goes down you stop thinking and move. Run . . . hit! Scott landed on top of the man, chopping the gun aside as they both hurtled into the room. He got a fast flash of Beth Frawley backed up against some file cabinets, holding a chair in front of her like a shield. Brief impression of a desk, lamp, phone, and then he and Buford were trying to strangle each other.

Talk about strong, the guy must be a wrestler in his spare time. Just missed with a knee to the groin, old trick favored by a certain tackle on the Montrose team. Scott got an armlock, but Buford broke it, hooked a leg through his and they rolled, thrashing and grunting. Okay, you want to get physical? Scott jammed a forearm against the throat; it gave him that instant he needed to pin the biceps. Man can't move with a hundred and eighty pounds planted on his arms.

Beth was coming to make an assist. She brought the chair down on Buford's head so hard it bounced. Then she raised it again. Puzzled, Scott watched as it came down this time straight at him. Instinctively, he ducked, so the blow struck to one side, but it flattened him. Gongs ringing, air full of black-and-white checkerboard . . . he felt his hands jerked behind him, wrists locked together. Handcuffs . . .

Still dazed, he could hear the girl's voice talking. On the phone? "That's right, you heard me," she was saying. "I nailed the kid all by myself. With that little creep from the CIA thrown in as a bonus."

ISABELL

□

"I STILL can't believe it!" Wedged between the two men in a tight mass of bodies and heavy coats, Isabell couldn't even squirm properly. "Beth Frawley, a terrorist?"

"Nothing else makes sense," Nighthawk said.

Abruptly Jonah asked him, "How did you tumble to it?"

The Indian heaved a sigh. "I noticed the girl back in Twin Forks. She seemed to be tailing the boy too—we were like beads on a string that Saturday. Then came the football game. She was rooting and cheering. I figured she's some sort of sports groupie, you know, worshipping the players. When she did make contact after the game, he gave her a polite brush-off. So I forgot about her until she turned up in Moab. Coincidences bother me."

"They don't worry you enough. You should have spilled all this yesterday." Then Jonah added grimly, "I might have been suspicious of the young lady myself if Miss McGill hadn't vouched for her."

Isabell felt a flood of color rising to redden her ears. "I've known Beth since she was a freshman in high school. She really did pursue her college career in the field of archaeology at the University of Nebraska. She wrote me once for a reference, when she was applying for a fellowship to go on a field trip to Egypt."

"Which is right next door to Libya," Jonah observed. "What do you want to bet she managed to get down to the Sudan, where it's easy to cross the border into Qaddhafi-land? Some of the deadliest of the hard-core guerrillas are trained there."

"But I know the child. She's bright, she's a very hard worker. Not just at school, but at home—she practically ran the house. Her mother works as a steno over in the courthouse. The father was an invalid, a coal miner—he finally died of black lung."

"Which no doubt gave her a leg up on her hatred of the power structure."

"Well, her brother was a very wild youngster, ended up in prison, I believe he died there. But Beth was smarter. She channeled her rebelliousness into schoolwork—her essays were brilliant. Usually on social issues, wickedly accurate when she tackled the evils in our society. I gave her good grades for it."

"How'd she get from sociology to archaeology?" Nighthawk asked.

"She said it was my influence." Isabell heard the dismay in her own voice. "I sponsored the after-school club for students interested in fossils, we called it the Stone-Hunter Club. I recall she once wrote a term paper on early cultures, how civilizations fell when they became decadent, using the fall of Rome to the Vandals. I remember that she rather applauded the Vandals. I guess I should have sensed the beginnings of a wrong direction." If it were true, if she had let Beth turn into a destroyer, it would be almost more devastating a failure than Fernando!

Nighthawk glanced across at her with concern. "Hey, you can't hold yourself responsible for every kid with a twisted mind. Basic values have to be taught in the home."

"You're right about that," Jonah muttered, following some personal train of thought. "How could they let a boy grow up addicted to a game? What were they thinking of, to let him put all the eggs in that one rickety basket? Do they even know that he's in this state of desperation?"

"I don't think so," Isabell said. "He doesn't let on. It's just that I've had some experience with—I recognized certain symptoms. The Drummonds are fine parents, very supportive."

"Yeah, they supported him to think he had to be a quarterback or die."

"Scott is a born athlete. They only encouraged him to follow his natural bent."

"That 'bent' starts the first time daddy shoves a toy pigskin into the child's hands. It builds up to the gift of a Mustang for winning the Triple A. Well, don't look so shocked—just because I haven't been on the scene in person you think I haven't kept track of my son's life? The football thing has worried me for years. Sure, I know all about the scholarship and the Heisman and how much money he'd have made in the pros. At age thirty he'd have been rich, if he hadn't already spent it, and stuck with a damaged body, nowhere to go but downhill into boredom. I wouldn't wish that on my worst enemy, much less my son."

"Well, the future is academic right now. Let's hope he's got one." Nighthawk was slowing the Bronco. "This is the town. Post office is in that shopping center."

"And there's the truck. I'll case the stores here"—Jonah

already had the door open—"and you go check out the rest of the town. If you see Steve, get him into the car, tell him anything on earth, but get him out of here. Don't worry about me. I'll hot-wire the truck if I have to. If you come up empty, we'll meet back here in an hour." He was out and gone, mingling with a group of men who were headed for the restaurant. White men in heavy clothes and hard hats, they looked like construction workers.

"He'll probably come out of there driving a bulldozer." Isabell could understand some of Scott's resentment. "The way the man gives orders, you'd think we were his servants. I happen to think we should have stayed together. Let's park here and join him."

"Not me." Nighthawk sounded amused. "When that fellow says 'Jump, Injun,' I jump."

"You're as good as a man as he is, any day." Mac McGillicuddy setting the record straight. "You weren't afraid to come back this morning and see if we needed help."

"Came to see you," he amended. "I figured he wouldn't stop you if you wanted to catch a ride home. As for the boy, that's between the two of them. They've got a lot to work out." He put the wheel over and headed out the road to the canyon.

"And they'll never do it with Jonah lording it. The man has no sensitivity at all. Or sympathy for what Scott's going through. The state of that young man's mind—when I think of it, I shudder."

"Yes, ma'am, I noticed." But the Indian wasn't being caustic. His dark eyes were warm with compassion. "You really are worried that he'll do himself violence."

"I saw it happen once before," she confessed. "I—I wasn't able to avert it. Where are we going now?"

He had taken a right turn onto a street of dirt. "I thought we'd skirt the town. Won't take long, you've already seen most of it." And in a minute he pulled off onto a flat spot overlooking a vast valley that stretched away to the south. Painted in ochres and siennas, it was dotted with small green patchwork where a few farms struggled.

"Is this the Canyon?"

"No, it's off to the east." He pointed to a rise of woodland. "That's the rim. My cousins are over there right now . . ." For a minute he fell silent, troubled. But when he spoke again, it was of Scott. "Suicide is a mystery to me. Death is such a darkness, where the *chindi* roams— all the worst part of what you were, alive. I was taught to dread it." Nighthawk shook his head. "Now if this was a Navajo boy, I'd know exactly what to do."

Isabell glanced across, wondering if he could possibly be facetious. But his slight smile was nostalgic.

"Indian child that grows ill in the head or the heart, you send for a singer. He comes and makes a beautiful sand painting, they sit the boy in the middle of it. Whole family gathers around—Navajos have hundreds of relatives, four, five times removed. Then the singer begins to chant. Sings about heroes, sings of the family and the whole history of the tribe and where you fit in. After a while you feel as if Changing Woman herself has reached down from the turquoise mountain like a long shadow to bring you a cool head. 'Now the child will go with beauty . . .' and everybody's happy. You don't know what happy is until it's multiplied by a houseful of Dineh."

The visual picture Isabell conjured brought an acute twinge to her heart. "The only family I ever had consisted of a mother who died when I was two years old and a father who derided every ambition I ever had. Silly dreams, of discovering long-lost civilizations. Of course, in a way he was right. The living world is the only battleground where you can make a difference. Or try."

"Teaching is the best way I know, to influence the future." Nighthawk looked toward the highway where a large modern building stood. "That's our Indian school. Little kids ride for forty, fifty miles to get an education. I'm glad your father didn't talk you out of that."

"He tried. I guess that's what drove me to it. He predicted I'd never like it or be good at it, so I finally dug my heels in and stood up to him." And spent the last eleven years of my life proving that he was right about that too! She sat speechless, choked on the truth. Glimpsing a larger revelation—that in his clumsy way, the Major had tried to save her from the devastation of failure. Had possibly even loved her . . . ?

Nighthawk was speaking half to himself. "Some of the old customs seem foolish to the younger generation, but there's wisdom behind them. The Dineh have a belief that you should never refer to, or even think the name of, a departed spirit. After a person's gone, you don't invite his ghost to hang around. It might come down your chimney hole and blow corpse powder on you and sicken you."

Isabell was startled by the words. Corpse powder? Yes, she had waded in it for years.

Diffidently, Nighthawk said, "You might feel better if you could nail a few boards across the door to all those memories." He was getting out of the truck.

Something told Isabell not to follow. She watched the Indian head for an outcrop of rock where stood a cairn of stones. As he reached it, he drew out the leather pouch and fumbled in it. With self-conscious dignity he laid something inside the shrine.

When he got back into the truck, his square face was slightly defiant. "Well, it couldn't hurt," he said. "I figure we're going to need all the help we can get."

JONAH

❑

ALONE, THANK God, this is more like it. Never did mesh well with other people.

Except Helene. Big dark eyes, remember the eyes, full of love. Like velvet when she told me she was pregnant. Such naked joy, seldom allowed to see into somebody's soul. She gave it to me like a gift.

Crazy, to have married her in the first place. Makes you so totally vulnerable. I can stand pain, death, so what? But I couldn't stand it if she were threatened with a scratch.

Now it's happening all over again with the boy. Eyes are blue like mine, but they've got her dark warmth. He has her grace. My bone structure beneath it, my blood pumping all that spirit through him. Young fool!

No, not stupid. He's exactly as hotheaded as you were at his age. You made a few mistakes yourself back in those days, old buddy. Let's hope he's got your reflexes for getting out of tight spots.

Plenty of guts, to come alone into this devil's den.

Hatred, tensions all around you like barbed wire. Bully-boy engineers at the counter, strutting their L.L. Bean boots, hard hats. Navajos like shadows back in the corner, blank-eyed, but they're centuries wise. Purebred Indian, not diluted like some tribes. Old men, young ones—are they some of the resistance force that's camped out at this canyon? Where is it, anyway? Ask the waitress.

". . . Canyon de Chelly?"

"Three miles." Poker-faced Indian girl, her eyes say *don't go*.

Finish the coffee and move out. Check the rest of the shops, while your neck hairs stand at attention. Stranger in town, who do you belong to, they wonder. Body knows when it's being watched, you get that slow burn in the pit of your gut—an ember fanned by each new draft of uncertainty. Anger, excitement, never sure what lies around this next corner—

Hold it! Over there, coming from that warehouse. Blood on his face, but I know the cut of the figure. Memories of Marrakesh . . . a dark street, the neon sign over the kooch joint, and why aren't there any Arabs lolling in the doorways? "I don't like the smell." Then Buford's cheeky smile in the glow from the sign. "You're just getting a drift from that dead cat in the gutter. Pike, you're strung out like a clothesline. Let me take this one. I could use a gold star on my file at Langley." It had been a trap, of course. Guns going off like World War III. All you could do was empty a clip and try to draw them off, over those cobblestones and up a wall. Didn't know the vine had thorns, took two days to pull 'em all out. Never saw Buford again. Until now—it was like picking up a loose end.

"Still walking into ambushes, George?" He's woozy—

get him back to the pickup. Put the tailgate down and roll old butterball inside, duck in after him and pull it up again. Windows in the shell are dirty, good. Hope nobody notices us.

"Johnny"—he's getting his breath now—"I'm too old for this. When a pint-sized girl can deck me—"

Damn! "Our Miss Frawley?"

"I don't know the lady's name, but she swings a mean chair. Of course she had some help from your son."

The spasm seizes you harder. Breathe, all the way to the bottom and let it out. "What about the boy? Where is he?"

"Dunno. He took me down, she finished me off. I just came to. That's been"—checking his watch—"almost a half hour ago."

They could be anywhere by now. "He thinks she's a damsel in distress."

"That'll be the day. She's one of the Shaman's protégés. At least"—Buford fumbles a handkerchief. Pour some water on it, mop off that blood—"I saw her in Twin Forks the day Holdrege got his ticket cancelled. Poor guy, all he was supposed to do was give us an assist, turn the boy away so he'd be forced to call you, bring you out of your hole."

"And then what? What's your assignment, George?"

"Recognition. They knew we were on the same team in Morocco. I was supposed to tail the kid until you showed up. Been all over the Rocky Mountain Empire. Was it you, the old wino in the park? Good cover. It only dawned on me later, after the kid acquired a white pickup, which I followed back to the motel. Ha, gotcha. You didn't know I was there. Of course, I didn't see you either. What'd you do, use the back windows? Then I saw the truck take off yesterday. As soon as I was sure where you were heading, I hung back. Too far, I guess. Lost you somewhere between there and here."

"What were you told to do if you found me? I mean, you couldn't take me on your best day with a backup of Ninjas."

"True. I was instructed to talk to you, offer inducements—anything you want if you'll just do a scan and point your pinky at our Shaman. We don't even have a composite of him."

"He's not here, George. According to my info he's in Bolivia, or maybe Chile by now."

Buford accepts. Moving on. "Rest of message: We could use your help. FBI tracked the Shaman's operation to this general area, but the Bureau isn't welcome down here. It's like an enemy camp. And not really their type of job, ferreting out terrorists. So any tips you've got, any ideas at all and we'll owe you big. Big enough to forget you ever had a son."

"Too late for that. It's already known to the other side, obviously. You've got a leak at Langley. With their usual finesse, the Company has put my son in danger, drawn me in where it's illegal for me to operate—"

"We're making it legal. Authorized at the very top level, Johnnie. Run any kind of mission you choose. I'm sure we're agreed on one thing: This New Year's Eve party must not be allowed to happen."

"My boy has top priority."

"Fine. We'll get him out of there. I think he'll be all right as long as they need him for bait. The girl may even go on playing fair maiden. Maybe that's why she left me alive, so as not to blow her cover. We can pick up the trail back at that building. I'll show you."

Sometimes you have to go along. Right now, you need him. So out into the chill again, down the alley to that warehouse. Along the hallway to a door still hanging open. A room that's empty. Office, just a front, impersonal. Empty. No, wait, over there on the floor—a fishing hat with a patch of sheepskin sewn on to hook dry flies in. It's Steve's, all right. Buford's found a stain on the cheap carpeting.

"That's where you went down?"

"No, I was over there." Points to another stain.

Everything heaves inside.

"Well, it explains why she didn't finish me off." George is on the same wavelength. It's obvious: he was supposed to lead me here. They might as well have painted a sign on the wall six feet high. WE'VE GOT YOUR BOY.

Steve!

SCOTT

❏

DUM-DUM, YOU didn't read the defense. Sacked for a
fifteen-yard-loss—that was some hit. Good thing I ducked.
Body seems operational, so it came through this time.
Maybe I'm not so fragile as those doctors thought?

Scott took inventory. Minor damage to the left wrist—
he calculated the nature of the pain like a connoisseur.
Plenty of flex in the joint, probably a sprain. Bruised it
when he went down hard, tackling Buford. Poor jerk.

No, I'm the flithead. It came abruptly, a rage so intense
it was like an extension of the headache that blazed in his
brain. Had to make like the Lone Ranger, charge in, save
the little lady. For a minute Scott was so mad he felt reborn
into a gut-kicker. He strained at the handcuffs pinning his
arms behind him.

A hard jolt racked him up and made him lie still. The
car had turned off onto a rough road, the bumps were
rubbing his face in the gritty carpeting. They had dumped
him in the back seat while he was still groggy, Beth and

some guy—phone call she made brought him fast, must have been hanging out somewhere nearby. They trundled him into this old junker Caddy. Stuck, stuffed, so what would Jonah be doing if he was in this mess?

He wouldn't waste time getting sore. He'd be taking notes. Where are we going? Road feels like do-it-yourself washboard, hard ruts, then sand. Scott squirmed over onto his side. Through the right window he could look up at a wall of rock that rose sheer, almost leaning out above them. Young-looking stone, it was clean as if it had been carved by a gigantic chisel in great slashes. Then the wheels splashed through water, the cliff was gone from the right and a new one towered on the left. So they had crossed a streambed and were going up the opposite side of a canyon. De Chelly?

They're taking you back to their camp, and nobody has a clue. You wanted to be on your own, you got it, turkey. You wanted a grand finale? It may not be an option anymore. Which is okay, except I'd like to take a few of them with me.

All at once the adrenalin was flowing, like the last minutes of the game when you're behind six points. Only this was fiercer. Greater. He began to understand why Jonah was turned on. When the stakes are life or death, it makes sports seem like kid stuff. Your whole mind is one red-hot chalkboard.

For instance, what can you do about handcuffs? Hard to argue with steel. Maybe if you look badly injured they'll figure you don't need them. So get the wrist to swell up good—lie on it. Harder. And keep your ears tuned, they're talking up-front.

Above the seat back he could just see the knit cap with the pompon. How he could have thought she was *cute*?

[117]

Beside her, the driver of the car loomed taller, heavy as a tackle, neck rising straight up to his ears. Black hair smashed down by a beat-up cowboy hat. Voice comes from inside a ton of chest. ". . . still think the world would be a better place with one less spook."

Then Bethie's little chipped tones, edged with authority. "Buford's no threat. He's long since over the hill, they had to pull him off a desk at Langley."

"Explains his pot. Man, I could play the rain dance on his belly."

"But he has his uses. He knows Pike from years ago— it's why he was sent out here. So when the fond daddy shows up looking for sonny-boy, Buford will make contact. He'll tell him we've got the kid, better than sending a telegram. Especially since we don't know Pike's current address. When he learns the story he'll come to us."

"You sure? What you told me, the guy's never even seen his son in his whole life. Maybe he don't care all that much."

She gave a snort of pure contempt. "It's Johnny Pike's one soft spot. He's absolutely hooked on the kid. Even pays a private eye to send him the football news from Twin Forks."

Scott tried to take that in. He wanted to unwrap it and stare at it and absorb it, but there wasn't time. They were talking on, up there.

"Don't need to tell this Injun how to hunt, little girl. Reason they call me Big Cat, I brought down a mountain lion when I was only twelve. You tie the bait to a stake— fat white rabbit, squeaking its head off. And then you sing the stalking song." He chanted a few weird sounds. "That means, 'Out of the darkness toward my feathered arrow he comes.' "

"Just make sure your 'feathered arrow' doesn't hit a vital spot. The Shaman wants some answers to a few questions. Like who his lieutenants are, the key to their codes, and so forth. Oh, I can't wait to have a chat with Johnny Pike."

"Don't worry, I'll take him alive. I got my own plans for that gent."

"It's not for you to make the plans." Beth is in charge, or thinks she is.

"Woman, this is my turf. Your boss wants the People to sign up for danger-duty, but you notice they didn't exactly rush around yet. You know why? Because you're trying to sell 'em a lot of hot air. The Dineh aren't dumb. They're waiting for your Shaman to show up so they can decide if he's the real thing."

"That's out of the question. He's got worse problems right now. He just had to get out of Ireland, Pike's men are all over the place like termites. He's gone to South America where our networks are being blown right and left. He's got to try to salvage what he can. So he's depending on me to make this operation succeed, and I intend to do it. My way. You got that?"

"Don't get ticked. I'm just saying if you can't produce a medicine man, maybe the People will settle for a demonstration of good faith. We give 'em Kit Carson."

"What's he got to do with anything?"

"You may know all about the Anasazi, but you didn't do your homework on our recent history. Like back in the 1860s, that's when old Carson was sent out here by Uncle Sam to exterminate the Navajo. He offered the ranchers two hundred fifty bucks a scalp. Burned our cornfields, killed our sheep, drove the Nation into this Canyon and slaughtered everybody who didn't give up. Not many things get the Dineh mad, but you speak the name of Kit

[119]

Carson, you better spit. So I'm gonna tell 'em Pike is another bounty hunter, sent out by the USA to knock off their leaders. I'm gonna give him to them like a burnt offering. Then maybe we got some volunteers for our 'holy cause.' "

Beth wasn't impressed. "The interrogation takes priority. When I'm done with Pike, you can have what's left, if it's still alive."

Scott swallowed down a wave of nausea. From the concussion? Or maybe another dose of the real world? Like being afraid for somebody else is a hundred times worse than being hit yourself. Comprehension was beginning to spread a fierce light inside him, getting brighter. This is exactly what made Jonah—

The car lumped to a stop and the engine cut off. Gametime. He did a fast psych job to get into character. Try to look pitiful, groan a little, make them underestimate. As the big Indian hauled him out, he made it a point to shiver. His teeth did their own chattering. Down in the shadows of the narrow branch canyon it was cold, though there was lingering afternoon sunlight along the main stem, which they had left a hundred yards back. He could see peaceful bottoms over there, with stands of bare cottonwood.

The gorge wasn't too deep here—four or five hundred feet—but the sides were sheer. It would take scaling equipment to climb out. Unless you could find a crevice? There looked to be a few fault lines in the rock face, deep enough to hold a remnant of snow from that last storm. Halfway up one wall a string of caves gaped as if one layer of rock had got tooth decay.

As Big Cat prodded him toward a cluster of tents, Scott saw a row of trucks nearby, a Jeep, and a car that looked familiar. Red Mustang, and on the shelf of the rear window a turquoise blue helmet covered with touchdown stars.

A rough hand shoved him along. "This ain't tourist season, sonny."

Beth had gone ahead into the large tent. When they came in under the flap she was pumping a Coleman lantern. The man pushed Scott down on the cot nearby. The tangle of blankets stank of cigarette smoke, stale beer, gun oil. As the lantern took hold he saw a dozen automatic rifles sheaved like cornstalks over to one side. Bandoliers of ammo looped across the top of the stack, and over by the desk an open crate was full of handguns, brand-new, wrapped in plastic. Other unmarked crates stood near a propane stove.

Big Cat scowled at them as he turned up the heat. "Where's that lazy Nicaraguan?" Going back to the tent flap he yelled, "Cruz! Get your tail in here."

The man who came slouching in was skinny, with the face of a muskrat. A straggle of moustache dripped off his upper lip like wet weeds. "You got the pee-jun, eh?"

"Yeah, we been doin' our job. Why ain't you done yours?" Big Cat jerked a thumb at the boxes.

"Hey, no sweat, mon."

"You sleep with this stuff next to your bed, we'll see who sweats." The menace in that tone made Cruz shut his wet red lips. Deliberately he ambled to the nearest crate. From the way he had to clean-and-jerk it, with a grunt, to hip level and then to his shoulder, it must be heavy. With what, Scott wondered—dynamite? Black powder? Or newer type stuff, gelignite or chemicals?

Big Cat had come across to sit down at the desk next to the cot, swiveling half around to face his prisoner. Same brown skin as Nighthawk's, but the eyes were odd—the color of dirty denim. Mouth crowded with choppy, stained teeth, stretched in a smile that only an alligator could love. Scott faked some anxiety.

"Good. You know who's who," the man said, "and we can all save wear-and-tear if you tell us where your daddy is."

"Clint?" Scott was trying to look stupid when the big flat palm connected. Illegal use of hands—hell, if that's the best he can do, he wouldn't make the team. But I'd better look as if I'm shook.

"No more games. Where's your father, the real one?"

"Oh. Him."

"Ri-i-i-ight."

"I wouldn't know. He hasn't been around since I was born. I wouldn't recognize the jerk if he walked in that door."

"You saying you never been in touch?" Too casual.

Scott saw some secret in the murky blue eyes and remembered Jonah's hunch about the wiretap on the phone at home. They could have been listening to every call for weeks. "Okay, okay, I called him. When it looked like I was being set up, I thought maybe he'd tell me what to do."

"So what did pappy say?"

"Told me to forget it and hung up."

"When's the next time you heard from him?"

"How could I? I've been on the run for corn-sake!"

Beth made a disgusted sound. "I knew it was a mistake, dumping Holdrege's body on the kid. I told you at the time—"

"Nah, nah, no mistake. He should have been tucked away nice and safe in jail like a good little rabbit. Lots easier for Pike to find him and us to find Pike. Now we got to send out the CIA guy like junk mail, who knows when they connect? Maybe never."

"Or maybe Johnny is already on the scene." Beth came over to study Scott like a frog pinned to wax. "There was an odd atmosphere in that motel, everybody fidgety, kept sneaking off into the bathroom. Did you have your old man stashed in the shower?"

Scott stared back at her disgusted. "How could he turn up in my room when I didn't know I was going to be there myself? I mean I'd barely hit town. I just ducked into the first hole I saw."

Beth showed her teeth in that slightly crooked smile that was really a grimace. "He's lying. I took psychology in college. When they look you in the eye like that, they're lying."

A shade of resentment darkened Big Cat's face at the word "college." Scott stored it for future use. But it wasn't divide-and-conquer time yet. The Navajo's mouth was hard as an arrowhead. He was fiddling with a metal paperweight—some paperweight, shaped like an oversized lemon and scored into squares. "Lemme ask you, sonny-boy: You ever thought what it would be like to die?"

When Scott laughed out loud, he saw an instant of surprise. But the word had been uppermost in his mind for so long, to get it out in the fresh air made him feel better. "Why not?" he said. "I was going to arrange it myself, but if you want to do the job, be my guest. Then you'll have to clean up the mess—that's the main thing been bothering me, who would have to deal with the body and so forth."

Big Cat frowned at Beth—what is this?

She said, "He's blowing smoke. If he had a death wish why would he be running for his life?"

"That's different," Scott explained reasonably. "Dying

is a snap. Living's not all that easy. Cops lock you up, people frame you for murders, or some little sweetheart of a girl slams you on the head, you turn into spaghetti. Sure, didn't you know? That's the diagnosis for my future—the next good hit and I'm a basket case forever. Why do you think I was only watching the game, Saturday? And without football, baby, I've got nothing."

For once her smart stuff came unbuttoned. Then she got it together again. "Dying can be difficult too. How do you feel about pain?"

He just grinned at her. "You mean in addition to my concussion, which feels like a hot bunch of shoelaces tied in knots? Plus my busted left wrist? And the knee that guy kicked when we were fighting? You feel like adding some more, you're welcome to try, but I reserve the right to pass out."

It got the handcuffs off. Big Cat examined the wrist and pronounced it only a sprain. And, Scott knew, there's always that next level of hurt, as in agony, which you don't shrug off. But for right now they were getting out a first-aid kit, fumbling with some athletic bandage.

"Let me do it," he said, "I'm used to this." By then the wrist looked really horrible, he was proud of it. And the bandage might come in handy—he used the whole length, crossing and crisscrossing.

"Come on, you're not gift-wrapping a mummy," Beth snapped at last. "Speaking of which, what happened to old McGill?"

"I hope by now she's back in Twin Forks teaching Beowulf to a lot of nice kids who will grow up to be highly educated black widow spiders."

That sort of tickled Big Cat. He was fiddling with the grenade again. Suddenly he bent forward to stare straight into Scott's eyes as if he were trying hypnosis. "Where . . . is . . . your . . . father?"

Goggling back at him, Scott said, "I . . . don't . . . know . . . and I . . . don't give a shuck."

Straightening, the Indian nodded. "I never had all the fancy schooling, but I was born with a gift. I know when somebody's telling the truth. And he is. Our rabbit. So why don't we sit back and relax."

ISABELL

❑

SHE WAS still angry at Jonah Pike! With his cold bitterness, thrusting that bent old fishing hat into her hands. The thing looked so symbolically dead—did he enjoy shocking her?

No, of course not. He was just working off his own anguish. Isabell could guess what he was going through as they stood there in the parking lot, Nighthawk and Buford uneasy, and Jonah rigid with frustration. Obviously it took all his will power to force himself to think analytically about the situation.

"Let's go have a look at the canyon." His words were almost inaudible.

The Indian looked dubious, shoulders hunched against the chill. "Might run into trouble."

"You'll be our passport."

"Also, it's quite a walk from the road, to get to that branch where—"

"So we'll walk."

As they headed for the Bronco, Pike was so preoccupied he forgot to try to leave her behind. The four of them had crammed in, Buford on the jump seat. Jonah had introduced him as "an old associate." Did that mean a spy? The man looked more like an automobile salesman. Pale, though, and rocky from a blow on the head—delivered by one Beth Frawley.

Isabell didn't want to think about her, but the sharp young face kept shoving its way into her mind. The memories of term papers—Isabell had thought them quite original, crisp ironic words, oddly slanted thoughts. She remembered one paper, on the farcical aspects of plea bargaining in our judicial system, heavy with cynicism for one so young. Beth had laughed it off, in their conference, she'd said, "Hey, my mom works as a court stenographer. She sees it all. The stories she tells—"

And then there had been the senior debate. Given, *Our Government: Right or Wrong?* "Please, Miss McGill, let me take the negative!" Beth's scornful oratory had made the referees uncomfortable—so many instances of "wrong," they should have given her the win. When they didn't, the girl had smiled, a strange, knowing smile. A really good teacher would have noticed, followed up on those early symptoms. But there was no time for self-castigation.

If I'm disillusioned, what must Scott be going through? To have been played for a fool, another blow to his self-esteem, driving him deeper into despair—at least he couldn't do anything drastic while a prisoner. Isabell refused to believe that they'd hurt the boy—they needed him. They would expect his father to come after him. And that, she realized, is exactly what Jonah will do. He's going to play their game.

Any lingering irritation toward the man drained away, leaving her weary and half-frozen. It felt as if hours had passed since they had parked and left her here in a dense thicket of stunted piñon pine with unyielding orders to stay in the car with the doors locked.

Nighthawk had given her a particularly earnest look. "Don't go wandering. Please."

She thought again about those few moments alone with him, the warming effect of his diffident words. To let the past go—she wondered if she could do it. Board up the old resentments, brush off the ghost powder? Maybe, if she could see Scott come out of this crisis, make some sort of peace with Fernando's *chindi*. Maybe then she could close the door on the Major and the entire past thirty-three years of her life.

But for every end, there must be a new beginning, and it's too late for that. Isn't it?

All at once she had to move, her blood was going into gridlock. She should have gone with them, should have insisted. Opening the door of the Bronco she got out, the hiking boots crunching the needles underfoot. Loud as the footsteps of a clumsy giant—the noise dismayed her. The men had moved with such easy stealth, hardly disturbing the stillness as they cat-footed away into the thickets of pine. Even that little roly-poly fellow in his brown over-coat—he was there one minute and gone the next like a woodchuck.

She clumped around the clearing, trying to revive her circulation. When she stumbled over a rock, she had to concede she would have been a calamity on a silent stalking expedition. You hate to admit you might not be right—the schoolteacher syndrome, to pretend you know best about everything on this earth. And the truth is, I don't know anything. Just maybe, though, I am learning.

"Maybe," she repeated aloud to a laconic white billy goat that chewed a weed as it stared at her. It hadn't been there a minute ago. Out of the underbrush another goat joined it. Then a whole harem trickled in through the dense thickets, white animals with long shaggy coats and strange, archaic eyes. A moment later she saw the boy, who also chewed. Unblinking, he blew a small pink bubble that burst against his lips.

"Hi, there," she said in her third-grade tone.

"Hi," he said distantly. "I heard you walking 'round. You lost or something?"

"No, just waiting. For some friends—some men. They walked over to look at the canyon."

The sudden grin was so broad it almost swallowed his narrow brown face. "Guys must be dumb, to put a fox like you on hold."

Isabell was flustered—she'd forgotten the glasses. Smiling back, she said, "What's your name?" And instantly damned herself for being rude, by Indian standards.

The boy didn't seem to notice. "Tommy Tsosie, only they call me 'Frog-lips.' Red Forehead born for Bitter Water." A lineage he'd been taught with his first baby words, like all Navajo children. "Of course I got a war name too, but I don't tell it. I bet you got no secret stuff. Whites don't have no fun."

"You sound as if you're pretty familiar with us." She noticed how his eyes met hers squarely. Parents of the old Dineh would have taught him this was bad manners. "I bet you grew up outside—away from here."

"Albuquerque," he said with pride. "My old man used

to work in a body shop, fix dings in the tourist cars. Wish we was back there. Wheels is where it's at, not goosin' a bunch of goats."

"But you can milk a goat if you're hungry."

"You kiddin'? My grandma'd lay words all over my skull if I bring home a empty goat." Then his black eyes brightened. "Course, maybe soon they'll let me in on the action. Like I told 'em, I'm skinny, I could get into small places and hide the—" He broke off.

"It's okay. I know all about the bombs. And the Shaman." She saw the word take effect. "I know exactly why you have gathered around the Canyon, just as the People did in the old days when their land was threatened." She was choosing her words carefully. It seemed like a golden opportunity. "But do *you* know what's going on in Congress?"

Frog-lips stood a fraction straighter. "I watch Dan Rather, sure I know. It's gonna be a law passed, kick us all out. That's why my old man brought us home, to fight 'em. So they can't take Dinetah, what else?"

"The 'what else' is just this: It hasn't come to a final vote yet. A lot of us are trying to block it. There are some powerful Senators on your side. But if you blow up a bunch of stadiums and hurt a lot of innocent bystanders, then nobody will want to help you. It will be the end of the Nation, while the Shaman flies off to safety. He's bad news, he's using you."

The dark little face was blank as the sky while the boy turned that over. Finally he chewed the gum again. "What's it to you?"

"I have friends who are of the People. I believe in right and wrong. I love this country, too, I want it to stay unchanged. So I hope your leaders will refuse to be taken in by the Shaman's promises. I'd hate to see your best men get killed."

It was the wrong argument. The child's scrawny face took on a shadow of pure valor. "Maybe it's worth it. If they gonna take our land, Lady, it's bottom-line time. A man's got to be ready to die for something, right?" He gave a short shrill whistle and the goats burst off into the pine thickets, Frog-lips after them.

A massive silence settled again over the clearing and the lone woman.

NIGHTHAWK

❑

AN EAGLE hung over the canyon, its fierce head twisting in search of small life in the grama grass far below.

Do not startle it. You are part of the tree.

Leaning against the warped cedar, Nighthawk hardly added to the long afternoon shadow it cast. Even if the people around the tents down there did look up, they'd only see another Indian. The two white men were well down in the brush. They were good at their trade. But the eagle saw them and tilted in a long skid that took it toward the main arm of the canyon.

This sacred place of legend, where Coyote threw his temper tantrum. Trying to make fire with flint stones, he didn't have the knack. In a rage, he threw them down so hard they split the earth in three long cracks, with many smaller fissures spreading out like broken pottery. You could still fit the pieces together in the eye of the mind. But he'd got his blaze, old Coyote, heat so fierce the earth began to boil.

Nighthawk looked down at the rock beneath his feet, frozen in undulations and swirls. He could almost feel the surging floods that had come to put the fire out, forcing the sides of the canyon apart so they could never be rejoined. And a slow joy began to blot out some of the frustration of these past years.

He felt a distant pity for that world back east where there was no amazement left. Where geologists saw a formation in terms of schists and stratification, their only interest the stains seeping down the rock face from those precious minerals they wanted to rip from the earth. And all the management types, with pockets so hungry for money—sit in those swivel chairs until they soften. A man ought to have good haunches. Lawyers—almost worst of all. Noses twisted with sniffing for tricky words to deceive the brain. And I passed that bar exam!

Nighthawk drew in a long breath of dry pure air, to clear his lungs of all the stenches of the "civilized" world. What I need is a singer to hold an Enemy Way for me. A full ceremony of praying and dancing (*restore me to health*). To ride wildly across the country on a plunging horse, carrying the rattle stick (*restore me to beauty*). To be blackened with the pristine charcoal of the cedar, as the Hero Twin had blackened himself so that he could creep up on the Yeitso—

But first I've got to help Pike slay his white man's monsters, for they have become ours, too.

Below, the ugly scatter of tents looked rotten as an infestation of maggots. Nighthawk didn't want to think about it. But to cure a disease you have to diagnose. He watched two men lounging near the row of vehicles. They wore combat fatigues straight out of a surplus store, long hair in twangs. One threw a beer can toward a litter of trash on the ground nearby. Strutting slightly, they walked over to pick up a couple of dirt bikes. When they revved them to life, the thin rackety sound reached the canyon rim faintly.

Jonah was following them through his field glasses. When they had gone down the track he swung the binoculars back to study the man who had just come out of the large tent. Massive, with the big shoulders of a Navajo, but somehow he wasn't put together right. His hips were too heavy and the legs thick; he lumbered like a wrestler. A dog rose from behind one of the Jeeps and trotted over to him, mixed breed, mostly hound, wagging a tail: Nothing to report.

Now the man was staring up at the opposite rim, or maybe at the caves halfway up the cliff. Nighthawk had noticed them. Nothing unusual in de Chelly, caves were everywhere, strung out like gopher holes. The People had hidden in them from their enemies in times long gone. Had died in them. A shiver traced a path along his spine.

Getting colder. Daylight was going fast, like a pink curtain pulled westward as the sun set. In a trick of the afterglow, Nighthawk suddenly saw a pattern. A rift in the canyon wall seemed serrated—a set of steps? A thousand years ago the Old Ones had carved footholds up these walls, leading to the caves. Great place to store beans and piñon nuts.

Or, he realized, practically anything else.

JONAH

◻

FROM THAT far side you could rappel to the caves, then work your way down that fracture in the rock, even in the dark. Which is why they have a dog. The minute it sounds an alert, first thing they'd do—

If they haven't already?

No, they'll keep him alive until they've got me. Keep him where? Not in the caves, too much nuisance, climb up there to feed him and all that. And yet they keep looking up. As if they're waiting.

Hold it, another one just appeared out of nowhere. Walking out of the cottonwoods at the base of the cliff, rubbing his shoulder, feet hurt. Surly. Points with a thumb upward: lousy caves. Jerks a head at the other two, revving their punk little bikes off down the track toward town. Ten minutes to four. Of course. Changing the guard. They've got a lookout down in the main canyon.

Rat-face is arguing with the big man, keeps waving at those caves. How many of them . . . nine . . . ten . . . eleven.

Hard to reach from below unless— Are those steps carved into the fault? If so, one of the caves is probably the munitions dump. Safe, dry, constant temperature. But which one? Impossible to tell where those notches lead.

Now they're all going back into the big tent. Is that where they're holding Steve? *Damn you, you hurt my kid you're crow's meat.*

Steve. We haven't even talked yet, haven't been on the same wavelength. Never dreamed it would be so hard. All these years I had so many conversations with the clippings. With his image, tagging along on stakeouts. Discussed everything on earth, philosophy, danger, tradecraft. Once taught him basic Russian that winter I was stuck in Poland. Never thought of him as a stranger.

Stupid, to expect him to take to me. What's to like, after all?

Cold ground sucks your body heat. Buford looks stiff as packing-house bacon. Getting dark, anyway. Give him the sign: Fall back.

Easy, in all this quiet the clink of a pebble would carry a mile. Show 'em how it's done, show the Navajos we've got some class. Oh sure, they're watching us. You can feel 'em out there in the forest. Weighing us against those others down below, waiting for some sign to help 'em make up their minds.

Say that again.

A sign. An omen. The right manifestation or maybe— the wrong one?

Got it, by God!

SCOTT

❑

SPORTS CLIPS, Jonah reading the Twin Forks *Gazette* over in Arab land—you got to be kidding. But why would Beth make up a story like that? So think. Try and think about the old man without chewing all those carpet tacks.

It was a relief for a while not to have any decisions to make. Cuffed to a cot in the small tent, Scott could catch his breath for the first time in days. Like Coach used to say, "Get orientated." Consider that it might be true: Jonah kept all that distance from you through these years not because he hated you, but because he—didn't. He didn't come here to catch the Shaman, he knows the guy is ten thousand miles away in South America. He's here to save your butt.

For you, he is going to come crashing down those rocks or crawling up the canyon, or maybe just walk straight on in with an Uzi on his hip, probably get himself killed . . .

No! Scott broke out in a sweat. As if a bank of lights had come on, he began to see more of it. All that talk about pain—the real torture would be to watch someone else get twisted, to hear another person scream. You moron, you stupid idiot, it was staring you in the face. Of course he had to cut out all those years ago. Because he cares. Not just a casual interest—he even knows how my "Gamebuster" works.

Scott had been confused by that reference back there in the Indian's shack. Thought it must be a trick. The old man had picked up the word from some remark of Gilly's maybe and was using it to impress him. There hadn't been time to figure it. Now, of course, it was obvious. The *Gazette* always turned the thing into a headline:

DRUMMOND PULLS THE GAMEBUSTER
WITH SEVEN SECONDS TO PLAY

Jonah must have read the whole analysis, to get the fine points. He knew it called for deception.

Deception—everything a quarterback does is designed to fool the opponent, but especially that call. You kind of limp out of the huddle like you're too tired to stagger across your own line of scrimmage—until you suddenly turn on the afterburners. Would that be a blast, if I could demonstrate it to Jonah in living color?

Except I wouldn't be around to hear the applause. So think about it one more time.

But what's to think? As soon as all this is over, I'd be back to square one, a little fish in a littler pond with no stats in the record book, none. You need to make some kind of hall of fame, even if you're the only one who knows about it. And this is the perfect good-bye—he could see a giant scoreboard with the numbers flashing. The kind of win that Mom and Clint—and even maybe Jonah—could carry around like a trophy to remember him by. "Our boy just wiped out a gang of terrorists single-handed, that's all." The sort of exit you've been looking for. No, no regrets.

Well, maybe one. Scott had to be honest—he wished now he could have had a few more days with this new father. To tell him a few things, so they sort of could understand each other. No wonder the guy never lightens up. In another burst of light, Scott almost laughed. On game day, you don't. You could break a toe on the astroturf and never feel it. Your best chick could elope with a ski bum, you wouldn't give it a thought. You're so high you could drop-kick the moon. And Jonah lives that way every minute of the year. The lucky dog. If I could do that I might want to stick around.

Forget it, you're not in his league. But you'd like him to know you're on his side all the way. Maybe he'll get the message, if you can just shape up a neat two-minute drill that will turn this game around. So let's get on with it.

First we have to get the wrist back in the lineup.

It was beginning to press against the handcuff. Beth's idea, to hitch the injured arm to the bed. "It'll make him lie still like a good little sacrificial lamb." Venom all over her face like slime on a cupcake—what's with her? But they could hardly get the steel ring closed over the athletic bandage, there was no room for further distension. Also it was warm in the tent, from the small propane stove and the Coleman lantern that hung from the centerpole, not to mention a few BTU's of his own that he was generating under the heavy Mac. So the wrist was swelling some more; what it needed was an ice pack.

Sitting up, Scott scrounged the cot closer to the wall, bringing his manacled left hand nearer the ocean of cold outside, held at bay only by the thin canvas. Old tent, the stitching looked worn. Maybe—

Abruptly the flap was flung back and the girl charged in. "What do you think you're doing? I saw you fiddling with the cot. The lamp throws your shadow on the side of the tent like a Punch-and-Judy show. Didn't know that, did you, peanut-brain?"

He blinked at her innocently. "You mean why did I sit up just now? Oh, thinking of you, I felt like I might puke."

"Very funny."

"I'll tell you funny," he said. "You won't believe this, but I actually envied you, being all turned on about archaeology. What a laugh. You could care less about having a great career. Proves a point I've been trying to make with my folks, that higher education is a crock."

It got under her skin, the elfin face soured some more. "What would you know about college? If it wasn't for all that muscle you'd never get past the front door."

"Better to have it in your biceps than between your ears. Anybody dumb enough to suck around some stinking Arab—" Then he knew he'd made a mistake.

Her eyes sharpened like a cat's. "So he is here! I knew it! No one except your father would be informing you about Arabs. And it wasn't over the phone—we've got a complete tape of that call you made."

"Not the one from the motel." Scott put on a disgusted look. "Yeah, I can be pretty dumb about people. I called him again, thought he might be interested that the cops are now after me. That's when he tells me this Shaman is a crazy Libyan or something. Said he'd take care of it over there in the Middle East. He told me to turn myself in, he'll see that I get sprung later. So he has no idea I've been suckered by a flirty little chick."

She gave him a smug smile. "Bugs you, doesn't it—to see a woman in charge? For your information, this is my mission. I planned it, I sold it to our leader—the archaeology cover, the idea of setting up a base here where 'government' is a dirty word. Sonny-boy, I am one hell of a guerrilla. It's what I was born to do."

"A shrink would say you're a born ding-dong. But then you know that, you said you took the subject in college."

She flushed as if he'd hit a sore spot. "What do they know, bunch of phonies, bandying their textbook words. They never deal with the basic vocabulary of life—poverty, exploitation, despair. And one of these days the underclasses will give new meaning to a few old goodies, like chaos and extermination."

Scott was fascinated, the way he felt in the reptile house at the zoo. "You really like the idea of killing innocent people? Suppose some of them are 'underclasses' too?"

"You have to break a few eggs to make a big upside-down cake. So long as we cancel out the guilty parties—like your stepfather, the oil baron. Got rich off manipulating oil prices so the poor people can't afford to drive to work. Hands out kickbacks, payoffs to the inspectors to overlook all the violations of the safety codes. So what if a few workers die?"

"Shove the propaganda," Scott snapped. "Clint never cheated or bribed or hurt anybody. You sound like some old Commie pamphlet."

"It's not theory, baby big shot. It's life. Y'see, my father worked for men like yours. He got crippling arthritis down the rotten shafts of those coal mines, standing water, foul air. His lungs were ruined by the substandard ventilation. And then they kicked him out to die by inches."

"Couldn't he get disability?"

"Another rotten joke. The government says, 'Hey, you're not disabled, you could run an elevator.' In a town where the tallest building is three stories high."

"So maybe you should have hired a lawyer to fight it."

She could have laughed if she could get her face un-clinched. "Lawyers are for rich folk. Us poor-offs have to settle for a public defender. Like the stuttering idiot who was supposed to represent my brother. Jack. Oh, I'm sure you never knew him, he dropped out of high school. But I bet he knew you and your pretty Mustang. Lord, how he drooled for a car like that. So what if he did borrow one, just to try it on for size? Was that worth a death sentence?"

"Don't give me that. They don't put people on Death Row for copping a joy ride."

"Oh, they called it one-to-five. But after a few months of hell in Canyon City, he caught a shiv in the back. While you were probably being handed an award for something like 'All-Around Best High School Snot-of-the-Year.'"

Scott felt a little sick. "I don't get it. What did I ever do to you?"

"You? You couldn't touch me, boy! You think it was any skin off my nose, giving me the cool shoulder that day in the parking lot after the football game? Big jock like you, wouldn't want to be seen with a girl who wasn't a total centerfold. Well, think again." Beth grinned furiously with those teeth that had never seen braces. "That was just part of the job, to butter up Johnny Pike's brat. When I want a date with an adolescent pretty boy, that'll be the day I blow my brains out."

After she'd gone, Scott lay there stunned. He had never been in the presence of anything that felt so lethal. Wrong, he'd been all wrong the way he was thinking this was some sort of game. This was the Evil Empire versus the Rest of Us. *And it's got to be stopped.* The final bank of spotlights came on, he could see the whole picture. This, this is what has been driving Jonah all these years.

After a while he managed to come in out of the glare of that truth. Back to the locker room and the chalkboard. The game had begun to diagram itself the minute he saw that grenade. His first thought had been how to target it. Couldn't take out the entire camp, but maybe if he eliminated the big Indian, he'd thought it might cause some confusion. Now the plan changed—it had to zero in on Bethie-girl.

In the distance he could hear her voice. "Cruz, get in there and take first watch over the prisoner."

"Me? You kiddin'? I been humpin' silly-putty halfway up that cliff all day, I gotta have some shut-eye, lady."

"I'll get someone to spell you at midnight. Just remember, all that beef is valuable, so keep awake and cut out the beer."

Scott wondered what Monster Slayer would have thought of an ogre disguised as a girl in a pink stocking cap.

Then the tent flap was jerked aside and Cruz came in, muttering Spanish profanities, sucking on a can of Budweiser. Glaring at Scott, he ambled over and gave the cot a vicious kick.

You can't take him with one hand pinned, so play it smart. "Hey, don't do that. It's not my fault she's a witch."

"You think she mean? Nino, I'm the Devil an' this is Hell, you got that?" Kick. "You see you' pretty car out there, eh? Well, ees mine now, so gimme the keys. I'm tired of hot-wirin'."

"Okay, okay." Scott dug them out of his pocket. "By the way, it has a dead body in the trunk."

"You tellin' me? Mon, I'm the hombre put heem there. Only now I left Mr. FBI back in the hills, feedin' some crows."

"Cops are looking for my license number."

"License ain't yours no more, ees off my ol' heap. Was shakin' to pieces, I follow you over them mountain roads that night, she leakin' oil like a tanker. Nice you leave your wheels just when I need." He stuck the keys in his pocket. "Now let girlie-face tell me I can't go to town."

Scott said, "Yeah, she'd make a great drill sergeant. How come a man like you takes orders from a woman anyway?"

"She ain't nobody."

"Oh. Then the other guy's the boss?"

"Big Cat? He's a damn Injun, he ain't nobody."

"Well, at least he's got a stake. I mean, what's it to you if the Navajos get run off their reservation?"

"Oh, Mon, you dumb. I hear they got no education them gringo schools. What I care about some Navvies? Don't you know we gonna bust the whole world? All them rich types, been stompin' us down, they gonna see. When it all blow up, we walk into them nice houses and take your mommy's diamonds, them silver forks you eat with, all that cash you got in the safe. I blow a safe pretty sweet, Nino. Yeah, this mon gonna have so much dinero gonna take a dive in it and never come up."

Half to himself Scott said, "So that's how she sold you. And you fall for it, let her run you around like a trained monkey."

"Shaddup!" Cruz kicked the bed again. "She don't run this mon."

"Yeah, that's why you're stuck here guarding me. Like I'm so dangerous, what a laugh."

The Nicaraguan's dark face hardened. "I'm just stayin' til she get her light off. Then I'm gonna sack out over my tent. But I got one eye open. You move, I see your shadow, I come here and kick you into tiny leetle pieces, okay?"

Scott squirmed and wiped the sweat off his forehead. "Listen, could you do me a favor? I'm about to die of thirst. How about you gimme a brew, huh?"

The Nicaraguan paused at the flap and drained his beer can. "Sure, kid, this Bud's for you." He threw the empty at Scott who could have intercepted it in his sleep. Instead, he ducked and the can hit the side of the tent to fall behind the cot on the floor.

As the man's footsteps died away, he lay motionless. You wouldn't think it would be that hard, to stay still. A pro like Jonah must practice it, lie there, listen as the minutes pass. In the distance a dog was barking, but not much. Probably tracking some small varmint. It would yip a wilder tune if a stranger tried to slip into camp. Don't do it, Jonah!

Surely the old man would be smarter than that. There were bigger stakes here than one life. No, he'd be figuring where the explosives are stashed and go after those. What kind of junk, dynamite? Or newer type stuff like plastique? "Humping silly-putty halfway up a cliff," of course, what else? Those caves. The perfect place. Only how am I going to get word to them?

Or maybe I should just rework my own plan. Must be complete boxes of grenades up there. All sorts of possibilities . . .

First things first. See if we can't let in some of that ice

from outside, get the wrist back in shape. Turning over, Scott felt behind the bed for the beer can, easing it up where he could go to work on it. With as little movement as possible he set his fingers around the top rim. Come on, Drummond, pretend you're in a commercial. He and Marhofsky had practiced it in the locker room with Pepsi empties. There's a knack, to crush as you twist . . . did it!

For a minute Scott held his breath, waiting for any sign that someone had noticed the sound of tearing metal. All quiet. Go ahead. He squeezed the ragged edges of the can together to make one double-edged cutter. Then he went to work on the stitching of the tent. Steadily, not pushing it. I've got plenty of time. The rest of the night. The rest of my life.

ISABELL

❏

Lying in bed, eyes closed, Isabell was vaguely aware of
an unfamiliar sensation. Not exactly hope, more like—
expectation. Remotely remembered as a fringe benefit of
childhood, it was a feeling she'd thought was long gone.
Drowsy, disbelieving, she reached out and drew it to her.
Expectation, or possibly a wishfulness, a warmth . . .

Beyond her eyelids she was aware of sunlight. What was
the comforting scent? Ivory shampoo—small luxury, even
worth Jonah's impatience. When they had stopped at the
convenience store last night it was written all over him: At
a time like this you want to wash your hair? But Nighthawk
had understood. He'd coaxed a few buckets of rusty water
out of the tank and hung a curtain beside the stove to give
her a modicum of privacy.

Isabell felt a rush of gratitude. Small favors she could
savor like the Navajo woman who had first lived in this
shack. The heavy comfort of the Indian's blanket was all
around her, like friendship. She waited for the echo of a

military snort of contempt, but heard nothing. Silence stretched like a whole new territory to be explored. Marvelous quiet . . .

Too quiet! Starting wide-awake, she bolted upright in bed to find herself alone. She remembered now the sound of the pickup driving off in the dark morning hours. Scrambling up, she went across barefoot on the cold linoleum to read the note on the table. Curt wiry handscript! *Gone to Gallup, back soon. J.* While she had snored on.

A burst of guilt scattered her euphoria. How could she have relaxed, with Scott still held by that gang of destroyers? And yet, as long as he was their prisoner he couldn't indulge in morbid impulses. Isabell realized that she was putting total faith in Jonah's ability to get the boy out. Which could be a mistake. After all, the man wasn't superhuman.

Hurrying now, she pulled on the wool slacks, the turtleneck which she had washed and hung near the stove. Briskly she laced the walking shoes, bought for those field trips with the Stone-Hunter Club. School seemed a thousand years away. She could imagine the gossip along the halls about now: "Old Gilly's disappeared, probably got murdered by a mad freshman she once flunked." "Maybe she eloped with a dictionary salesman." Giggle, giggle. "Poor jerk better know all his parts of speech or she'll assign him extra study halls." "You kidding? Gilly wouldn't know what to do with a guy's parts of speech." Shades of a conversation once heard on a crowded bus.

She laid down the cheap hairbrush and began to gather the shining mass of hair into a tight coil. Then, in the scrap of mirror, saw Nighthawk standing in the back door behind her with a look of protest.

Turning, she smiled uncertainly. "Hi."

[148]

"*Ya-tah-hey.* You look great this morning." But his dark eyes said, Don't go back to yesterday, please!

Why should it matter to him? Flustered, she let her hands fall to her sides, leaving the long locks to fall loose around her shoulders. "Old cliché: can't seem to do a thing with it."

Shyly he said, "No need to pin it so tight unless you're going to pick corn maybe." Teasing, to cover a slight embarrassment as he took a folded bundle of tawny fur from under an arm. "Found this for you. My grandfather made it for my grandmother. She got tired of those hard boards—" He jutted his chin toward the distant outhouse. "It's badger skin."

Holding it up she saw the pelt had a large hole cut in the middle and laughed. "Thank the Lord! I was beginning to think that Indian women were made of iron. I felt like a sissy." Then she realized. "You went inside the old hogan? Doesn't that trouble you?"

With a sheepish twitch, the Indian said, "Some, I guess. Grandmother died in there of a heart attack, gone before they could carry her outside. When you're brought up superstitious you can't help notice things. Like when you hear an owl in the night. And then this morning, where the snow left a wet spot on the north side of the hogan, I find fresh coyote tracks." He shivered slightly and picked up a stick of wood to put in the stove. "I've been feeling spooked ever since we were at the Canyon yesterday."

"It even seemed to disturb Jonah. But then," she added, "it's hard to tell. He and that Buford, they talk in a sort of verbal shorthand: 'Disinformation.' 'Misdirection.' And 'not viable' and 'calculated risk.' I was too sleepy to figure out what they were cooking up."

"Don't ask me. I didn't make the all-pro spy team. Whatever it is, Pike's going in there for the boy. Can't blame him. Only somebody has to focus on finding that ammo dump, which leaves me. I can't let the People get mixed up in a no-win situation for the benefit of some Libyan kook."

As she began an experiment with braids, Isabell said, "Didn't I hear Jonah speculate that their arsenal might be hidden in a cave?"

He nodded. "Up above the enemy camp, a whole string of them. Eleven, to be exact—ideal place to store munitions. Looks like there may be steps leading up a fault in the rock, but you can't tell where they go. The rift is deep and well-guarded at the bottom. I could shinny down a rope from the top if I knew which cave to aim for."

"And if you did find it, what would you do?"

"Try to blow the works. They can't have their New Year's Eve party without their thunder-stuff."

"Why don't we just alert the army and let them march into that place and wipe the gang out?"

"Not so easy. The terrorists hold a strong position at the mouth of a narrow branch canyon. Plenty of fire power to stave off an attack."

"But the soldiers would have the high ground on the rim."

He shook his head. "Rim belongs to the People. They're all over the place, waiting for this Shaman to show so they can make up their hearts whether he's the real thing. If they see troops come through the woods, they'd jump fast—the wrong way. In a war between the army and the Navajo, nobody wins except the crazies. The government would look like a bully, the Indians would lose lives, maybe lose some of their support in Washington if they take down a lot of whites. Meanwhile the Shaman's people slip away to set up again somewhere else. No, the best thing to do is blow that dump, buy us some time. At least I've got to try."

He loosened his belt and brought out the leather medicine pouch. Laying it on the table he spread it open to sort through the contents. "Most of this stuff is too potent for me. Grandfather left it to me because I was the oldest and nobody else in the family had any gift for the spiritual. He thought I showed some promise. But I lacked the patience. You have to learn hours of chants, can't have a word wrong. Know all sorts of sand paintings down to the last sacred grain of sand, no imperfections except the one you make on purpose, to keep from getting too prideful. Takes years, makes Harvard look easy. No, I'll never be a singer, but"—he glanced at her with a touch of diffidence—"I used to be a pretty fair hand trembler."

NIGHTHAWK

❑

THE INDIAN blanket spread in the center of the kitchen floor gave the shabby room an aura of dignity. In patient browns and grays with a pattern of black-and-white triangles, it radiated the pride of the weaver. Nighthawk stepped onto it reverently. He had stripped to jeans and would have taken those off too if he had been alone.

The woman—privately he called her "Tall Dove," with that graceful neck and the alert tilt of her head—stood apart hesitantly. Finally she came out with it. "Would you rather I'd leave?"

"No." It surprised Nighthawk. He'd thought that he did wish it. But all at once it came to him that her presence reinforced him; that would have to be thought about later. It had rarely happened, and never with a white person. Especially not a woman.

He was very aware of her, sitting off to the left like a warm rock, reflecting the sunlight in the room. He tried to include her as part of the ritual. Concentrate: This is your litmus test, to see whether you're still a Navajo.

From the medicine pouch he had taken a small blackened sliver of wood, cut from a lightning-struck tree. But at the last minute he set it aside—not for a novice to use. The bit of turquoise was safe enough. Good luck to hold a piece of sky in your hand. And a packet of corn pollen, that was a necessity. The bit of cedar carved into a mouse shape he recognized as his grandfather's own fetish. Gripping it now, Nighthawk tried to visualize the old man's face, to hear the patient voice giving him instructions. But that was so many years ago, and I was so young.

Come on, Mouse, how does it begin? With a prayer, of course, but which one? To locate sickness in a person you appeal to Black Gila Monster. Only what if it's a canker of a cave? He laid out on the blanket in a row the eleven pebbles. He had gathered the darkest and flattest he could find, arranging them now two and four and one and four, like the openings in the canyon wall. Mouse, scuttle up those cliffs and take me to the evil one. (Or I'll subpoena you!) The dust of swirling identities almost blinded him.

Concentrate. Look at the pebbles and—what? What do I do next?

Sweat trickled down his ribs. It occurred to him that he hadn't used his Speed Stick in days. A terrible frustration almost wiped him out. You are home in Dinetah where the functions of the body are part of the beauty of nature and cannot be offensive. Now get on with it!

A prayer. But which one? He had once gone to an Episcopal church. In the middle of the doxology he had thought of White Corn Boy and prayed to him for the gift of crops. Was that so bad? As long as the words come from the heart, what difference? If you can't remember the right ones, try any that come to mind, but do it!

"The feet of the earth are my feet . . ."

(That isn't how it starts. Never mind, keep going.)

"The legs of the earth are my legs . . ."

(Your honor, I must object. What exactly does that mean?)

In a burst of desperation Nighthawk mentally burned every law book he'd ever read. He shut his eyes and tried to picture the ground beneath the floor of the old shack. To sense the layers of rock stratified below, deeper and deeper, on down to the raw magma.

"I am the sacred words of the earth."

And very slightly some current moved in him, spreading slowly upward and outward into his arms. Time for the pollen. He took the small packet and poured the yellow dust into his palm, a pinch to each corner of the blanket, and rub the rest on the backs of your hands. He shut his eyes again and stretched out his arms. Don't force it, let it happen . . .

"The voice of the earth is my voice."

In his fingers he began to feel a strange tingling as his hands began to move. Slow to the left, back to the right, of their own accord they swung in low arcs above the row of stones. And each time, at some point he felt a pull in the right, like a magnet passing over a scrap of iron.

"The strength of the earth is my strength . . ."

Abruptly an irresistible force gripped his hand and drew it down hard. His fingers closed around one of the pebbles.

When he opened his eyes, Nighthawk was dazed to find himself the center of an audience of three. He hadn't heard the men come in. He hadn't even felt their skepticism. And then he realized that in their hard eyes there was no mockery. It was as if each was recalling some unexplained experience from the past, even from another part of the world.

With a slight shrug Jonah said, "Fourth cave from the right." And Buford nodded.

Tall Dove was smiling as if she just invented happiness.

JONAH

□

Aᴍ I wrong? Maybe the caves should be my primary objective. Is fear for the boy clouding my judgment? I don't think so. Propaganda could be a crucial factor in the overall picture.

No time now for uncertainty. Buford keeps giving me looks, so ungrip the wheel and stop sweating. You'll get your feathers damp.

Plenty of itchy disguises in my time, but this one takes the cake. Haven't put the headpiece on yet—don't want to draw attention, some shaggy bird-thing driving down U.S. 191 in a pickup.

Whole scheme is hairy, but will it work? It's got to. Steve—! If anything happens to him what do I say to Helene?

"By the way"—Buford is a mind reader—"I met your wife. Lovely, gracious woman. I can see why you had to cut the family ties; it does increase the risks. Like right now—forgive me, old friend, but you're not displaying your usual hard-nosed practicality. This scam of yours has odds only a drunken bookie would love."

"Nobody asked you to deal yourself in. In fact, why don't I let you off in town, you get in your car and take a very slow route back to Langley. Tell 'em you lost me."

"Can't do that, Johnny. I'm happy to let you run the show your own way. But if you get wrecked somebody has to call in the cavalry. Don't glare at me, you know we can't let that gang of spoilers walk out of here to sabotage the country at will. They've got to be stopped, even if that pretty little canyon becomes a slaughterhouse."

"You're out of your jurisdiction."

"Obviously. The FBI ought to be calling the shots. But so far they only have one man on the scene and he shows signs of going permanently native. Singing songs to a bunch of rocks—I noticed you weren't laughing."

Hardly. Seen too many strange manifestations, especially that winter hiding out among the Tibetan tribes. A lot of things we don't know about the powers of the mind.

"Me neither," Buford was going on. "I spent a couple of years in Haiti, posing as an importer. Down there they've got what they call Obeah—voodoo. Can't say I care much for it, but I don't knock it."

Never underestimate the power of a man's beliefs, they're what makes him tick. Just hope the Navajos are as committed as Nighthawk says. He swears they're totally fastidious about their mythology.

Can I count on that?

Can I count on him to bring them out of the woodwork in time?

Can I pull this sucker off?

SCOTT

❏

GREAT SCRAMBLED eggs, greasy as ball bearings. And Big Cat watching every move with those muddy blue eyes—distract him. Maybe if I get him mad? But not at me, I don't want him yanking me around, he might see that ripped seam. The loose canvas was hidden by the cot. Scott just hoped nobody would feel the sneak of cold air along the floor of the tent.

"You ever meet the Shaman?" he asked, chomping a piece of half-burnt bread. Awkward, eating with your left hand linked to the far side of the bed. He made himself look as helpless as possible.

Big Cat considered the question, decided it was harmless. "Uh-uh."

"Guess he's got bigger fish to fry. You do know he's an Arab."

"She said you'd try to pull that one on me." The Indian's eyes narrowed to slits. "Don't matter, I don't care if he's a monkey's brother-in-law, his money buys powder and shot."

"Shot?"

"That's a joke. In the old days, when the Dineh fought the Spanish, it was buckshot did us in."

"Us? You actually a Navajo?"

The swarthy face darkened to an off-shade of red. "Listen, maybe some blue-eyed soldier knocked up my great grandma, that don't make me a mongrel, sonny-boy."

"I didn't mean that. I just thought an Indian wouldn't get his own tribe in the sheep-dip, not for an Arab or his girl friend. Where is Betty Coed, anyway?"

"Gone to town, to call the boss—South America or wherever. And for your info, kid, Big Cat don't work for nobody but me. I got my exclusive contract."

"Better read the fine print. Those college kids know all the tricks."

The eyes dulled like an overcast sky. "I see what you're up to, but it won't work. That little babe writes a beautiful check. She's got the connections to buy everything up to an A-bomb, she's okay by me. Maybe when the fireworks is over I get rid of her, but right now I need her. So eat up, I got other stuff to do."

Scott hesitated over the last of the scrambled eggs as they heard the sound of footsteps running.

Cruz burst into the tent. "Hey, mon, you gotta come queek. He's here."

"Who?"

"Ol' Shaman in person weeth all hees feathers on. You gotta see thees."

With total cool, Big Cat came over and picked up the empty plate before he followed the man. Scott lay back with a handful of greasy eggs which he shoved in his pocket as soon as they were gone. So far so good, if this new development didn't complicate things. Somewhere in the near distance a confab was going on. He could hear Big Cat's barrel baritone.

"Your little soldier-girl ain't here, and I don't know you from Old Man Coyote. You're going nowhere until you gimme some proof. What kind? I dunno . . . tell me where the ammo is stashed. If you're really the Shaman you'll know."

". . . cave . . ."

"Which one?"

"Fourth from zee right-hand end." The other voice came muffled with some sort of accent.

A grunt. "Okay. Sorry if I gave you a hard time, but you gotta understand—the truth is, mister, your get-up is a crock. It ain't Navajo, not any of it."

Another mutter.

Then Big Cat said, "Maybe so, but the Dineh are gonna split a gut laughing, they see you in that junk. Some of it is Hopi kachina and some of it's Zuni Shalako and all of it's fake. Looks like you raided a tourist trap down on the big highway. Nothin' to me, but if you wanta sell the People on joinin' up, you don't want to look ridiculous. Better stay outa sight while I rustle you some *Yei* duds. I packed some along in case I had to do an act of my own. Sure, go talk to the prisoner. He's in there. And don't come out till I get back, huh? Cheez, I hope nobody saw you."

The tent flap lifted then. Ducking in under it came a wild figure dripping bangles and beads and shells, its head topped by a huge spray of black feathers that shot out in all directions. The face was red and black and twisted in the middle by a white grimace of familiar dentures.

Scott grinned back. "Don't look now, but you're moulting." The surge of gladness confused him. He even imagined Jonah looked pretty pleased too.

"If you're implying that this disguise is a turkey, it's supposed to be. I gathered up the worst junk the curio store had to offer. How'd you make me so fast?"

"Never try to lie through those teeth."

"Well, I'll be damned."

"Listen, though, bloody queen Bess may be back from town any minute and she knows the real Shaman. She may even be talking to him right now, so—"

"Let's hope she gives us some slack. Nighthawk is up on the rim trying to turn out the Navajos, telling them the big medicine man is on the scene. I want an audience and they're not there yet."

"You're playing to the crowd?"

"All the way." He stuck the rattle under his arm and dug inside the costume, batting feathers out of his way. "Symbolism is a strong force with these people. I'm hoping if they see a mix-and-match phony strutting around down here it will turn their stomachs. Meanwhile, do you know how to pick a lock?"

"Gee, no, it was one of those electives I didn't take."

"Let me have a crack at it. What's with the wrist?"

"I sprained it slightly. No problem, the swelling's gone down." Soaked in icy air all night it was almost back to normal.

Jonah fiddled with the pick and swore, searching for a different shape in his pocket. From the distance came the sound of wheels skidding to a stop on hard gravel. Smothering a word, he slicked his feathers and was back on the other side of the tent as Beth thrust through under the flap, looking too small for the .357 Magnum she was holding.

"Well, what do you know," she marveled. "It worked."

The bird figure turned fiercely, but the gun didn't waver. Both her hands were clamped on it like a small white interlocking vise. "Mister Pike, I presume." With a terrible smile she tracked Jonah as he circled the far side of the tent.

Scott dug the crushed beer can out from under his hip. Caught Jonah's eye, and with one fast fling, he stuck it in her ear. As if they'd practiced it a hundred times—Jonah kicked the gun out of her hand and moved in to chop her neatly across the neck. She dropped like old sweat socks.

"You're a natural at this." Jonah was back at the cot fumbling his lock picks.

"Don't mess with it," Scott urged him. "I'll be okay."

"I'm not leaving here without—"

"Dad!" The word jolted them both. "It's showtime! Go on out there and strut your pompons. I have my own plan," he yelled softly. "If you don't let me handle it you'll ruin everything."

His father hesitated. That inexplicable "everything" hung in the air between them like a challenge. Or a promise? After a long second, Jonah nodded his topnotch and ran for the door, scooping up Beth's cannon on the way.

By God, he trusts me! Scott was rapidly unwinding the athletic bandage on his wrist. He paused as the girl began to stir. She floundered to her knees, scrambling across the floor, looking for the gun. When she couldn't find it, she clawed out a smaller revolver she'd been wearing under her parka. Still fuzzy, she aimed it straight at Scott.

He made himself sit still and look stupid, hoping the lengths of elastic wrap were hidden by his Mac. In his best idiot voice he said, "Hey, point that somewhere else."

Shaking off the fog, Beth lunged up and out of the tent. Quickly he finished his job—the handcuff was loose now around his wrist. Digging in his pocket for the wad of eggs, he rubbed the bare arm and hand with them. Outside, the girl was yelling for her troops, sounds of confusion, shouts. He could picture Jonah doing a broken-field run through the camp. The dog was barking up a storm, but no shots yet. She would want to take him alive. *Give Jonah an inch and he'll take the whole nine yards. I hope!*

With a hard yank Scott pulled his hand through the steel ring. Then dove for the slit in the tent, worming his way into fresh air. High noon, the sun was shafting straight down into the canyon. It was a beautiful day, so perfect it almost gave him a qualm of doubt. But it was too late for second thoughts.

He needed to formulate a new strategy, centered on those caves. Now that he knew which one to target the only question was whether he could reach it with a long Hail Mary. *Hard to judge proportions in a setting so big. Not like a football field where everything is marked off by tens. Hard to see the caves from right below them. Get a better idea from across the canyon.*

He ran for the line of vehicles and crouched down behind them, working his way toward the big tent. He could hear a scramble going on inside, guys grabbing those automatic weapons. *Don't take the grenade, please!* Scott paused behind an old friend. *Good car, the Mustang. Sorry to say so-long to that.*

Now they were all kiting off down the canyon. *Jonah, leg it!* The intensity of that wish almost swamped him. *Those five minutes, just the two of them alone in the tent, were greater than anything he'd ever known—like on a different plane. The world seemed to move faster—game day, only better. If it could always be like that, I'd stick around. . . .*

Too late. Too late. Beth was screaming in the distance, must have decided better-dead-than-fled. A blast of gunfire sent wild echoes bouncing around the canyon. The noise steadied Scott. He always did brace up when the amplifiers began to boom out the lineup, crowd roaring at every call. Glancing up at the rimrock, he realized it was alive with Indians. They had come out of the woods, a hometown audience waiting for something to cheer.

So let's bust this game wide open. On the count of three, hut . . . hut . . . hold it!

As he came up out of his crouch, Scott caught a glimpse of turquoise. The uniform was still where he'd dumped it in the back seat that night so long ago. Yanking the door open, he pulled it forth. Dazzling, brilliant, with silver lightning stripes down the shoulders and the mystical number "8" looming large. A helmet full of stars like a ceremonial mask. So symbols mean a lot to the Navajos?

Monster Slayer, eat your heart out.

ISABELL

☐

LYING FLAT on the rimrock, Isabell felt as if a whole handful of E-Z-Lite charcoal was smoldering in her midriff. Face scratched by the scrub pine, smudged with stovepipe soot for camouflage, she felt totally alive for the first time in years. And illogically pleased with herself, to have impressed Nighthawk.

He hadn't wanted to bring her along until she had mentioned offhand, "I have a friend out on the rim who might help us reach the men hidden there in a hurry." And when she'd called out for Frog-lips and the child came—suddenly again out of nowhere—the look on Nighthawk's face still made her laugh inside.

"Ol' Shaman's comin'? No joke?"

The Navajo boy had known exactly how to spread the word. Within minutes of the time the two of them had disappeared into the woods, the Dineh had begun to materialize along the canyon's edge. Blending with the gnarled forest they looked as if they'd just risen from the raw earth—more and more of them, watchful, curious.

The silence was massive. Not a sound sifted up from the bottoms where a few men lolled in front of the tents and the dog excavated a gopher hole. Across the canyon the row of caves were black-shadowed as openings to a nether world. In that brilliant light she couldn't see the steps, but obviously anyone trying to climb that cliff face would be an easy target.

So maybe Jonah was wise, to go for the stage effect and try to discredit the Shaman myth. And of course, to free Scott. What this must be doing to the boy, driving him to what new ends of despair? Isabell swallowed on a dry throat, a long gulp that made the nearest Navajos turn and look. She shrank lower in the brush. The People would never hurt her, but they might make her leave.

Then in that vast stillness a sound came distantly, the slow grind of gears as the Bronco came rocking along the uneven track, flanked by two scruffy motorbikers, who led the way into the branch canyon and motioned the driver into a grove of winter-bare cottonwoods some hundred yards below the camp.

A weird figure got out and started to walk the rest of the way, flopping his topknot and waving his rattle at the dog who came racketing. Isabell saw several of the Navajos focus binoculars on the scene below. The glasses got passed around and she caught the mutter of words exchanged. Up and down the rim, Indians were leaving the shelter of the woods to come forward for a better view.

Below, a big man in a cowboy hat was hurrying toward Jonah, ushering him quickly to one of the smaller tents. As a prisoner? No, there'd been no menace in his movements. When he came back out alone, his confederates gathered around him in a cluster. Laughing? The Navajos were not amused. It's difficult to read an Indian's body language, but she thought they seemed affronted—stiff as prairie dogs that sense a predator.

And now another vehicle, a Jeep, came bouncing and rocking up the track. It slammed to a halt and a small figure leaped out, a girl in a ridiculous pink stocking cap. After a few seconds' confab with the men, she turned and ran to one of the tents, back at once with a gun that looked huge even from this distance. She plunged into the small tent, and it was all going wrong, Isabell realized with dismay. Jonah had lost his gamble. Now there was only Buford to save the day, but the man just sat there in the Bronco. Her hands clenched—coward, coward, coward!

The scene below seemed frozen in time, as if the men were uncertain what to do. When all at once the scarecrow figure with its strutting topknot erupted into the sunlight and scampered crazily past them, away down the track.

In a minute Beth staggered out, minus the pink cap— she waved to the others: Catch him, you idiots! But Jonah had a good start, for all his clowning. He kept up the caricature of fear—when the dog snapped at his heels, he jumped in the air and threw his rattle at it. The mutt fell back with hurt feelings. Only when the men came pounding in pursuit with their vicious weaponry did Buford suddenly ram the Bronco up the track swinging the vehicle in a circle past the "Shaman" who leaped onto it, riding the rear bumper in a getaway reminiscent of the Keystone Kops.

Meanwhile Isabell was dividing her attention, as she saw Scott slip from the back of the small tent and duck across to crouch behind a red Mustang that looked familiar. She'd wondered what on earth he was up to, seizing an armload of football gear and dodging into the larger tent, now apparently deserted. But a moment later she understood.

A different personage stepped forth to take center stage. Mighty-shouldered in celestial turquoise—does he know that the number eight has special meaning to a Navajo?—wearing a star-studded helmet, the superboy began to march up the canyon like a crusader. Having lost the Bronco, some of the gang down there were coming back—they'd spotted him, raising their terrible semiautomatics. But Beth shouted at them to hold their fire. Bless the girl! Then as she raced past in pursuit, she snapped off a shot with her own huge gun and it came clear. The little witch! She wants the kill herself!

Isabell swallowed hard, a wave of nausea. She had never before hated a youngster, someone she'd taught—

The turquoise figure had broken into a jog, that evasive Drummond wolftrot that made sophomore girls swallow their bubble gum. Confident, untouchable, glancing back almost casually, he noticed Beth. She was running, shooting again. Isabell saw the pistol jump, then heard the distant report.

CRACK!

Scott had jinked to the right. The ESP that had preserved him so often from the blitz, that made his teammates claim he had eyes in the back of his head, seemed to be functioning. He zigzagged left and right and again right just as she got off the next shot.

CRACK!

Moving up the canyon at a diagonal, he was holding a small object that glinted in the sun. And suddenly Isabell knew what it was. But what on earth could he do with a hand grenade?

CRACK!-zingggg. Ricochet.

That's four. Isabell hadn't realized she was counting.

Now five. Then Beth seemed to realize she wasn't taking enough time to aim. She stopped and steadied the gun with both hands.

CRACK!

Scott had dropped to a crouch. He didn't even look up at the bullet-chipped rock above his head. He was staring across at the caves as he fiddled with the lethal thing in his hand while Beth jammed home a new handful of shells as fast as she could reload.

The boy straightened now and headed across toward his target at a hard run, and all at once Isabell understood. No! She almost screamed it aloud. *No, you can't make it!* Even you can't throw that high and far.

Scott realized it at the same instant, with his right hand cocked to throw. He had misjudged the vastness of the canyon, the height of the cliff. Stopping in his tracks he stood with sloping shoulders, telegraphing defeat. While Beth took deadly aim. It was all over.

NIGHTHAWK

THE INDIAN was sweating as he inched his way down the face of the cliff. The scenic route. Frog-lips had shown it to him— "Hey, it's a piece a' cake, brother." And there was a time, Nighthawk thought, when he would have said the same. But these fingers haven't gripped anything rougher than a #2 pencil in years. The handholds were jagged and the cracks might possibly be big enough to hook a toe in, if the toe was bare. But he was going to need the boots at the bottom, to cross the canyon and make his way up the other side to the caves. If he got that far.

Over his shoulder he could see the camp down there in plain view, but everyone was running the other way, waving a lot of artillery. Better hurry, I might be needed. It never had occurred to Pike and Buford to ask for backup. But if things went wrong, who would haul the boy out? And the kid means so much to her, to Tall Dove . . .

Nighthawk dropped the last few feet to the sloping scree, turned his ankle and rolled to the bottom. Really graceful.

Scrambling up, he moved toward the camp at a fast limp, trying to blend with the brown rock. He could hear shooting now, wished for a gun himself, and then was glad he didn't have one. The thought of killing made him sick. Some G-man. He was about to head for the caves when he saw an apparition in turquoise emerge from the big tent. It jolted him to a standstill.

Fabulous in every sense—the figure clad in invisible luck was straight out of folklore. Trotting along with the bullets singing . . . Of course, like every other Navajo in the vicinity, Nighthawk knew with one part of his mind that this was a youth dressed in a football uniform. But the vision seemed to grow taller, brighter. The stuff of myths is man transformed into a holy spirit for an instant of glory. No reason the gods shouldn't wear shoulderpads.

So long as they don't do anything ridiculous! As he saw the arm come up, he realized what Turquoise Son was holding. No, no, no, he prayed, don't even try! He saw the boy check, as if he too realized the impossibility. And in the near distance the girl was aiming a gun.

CRACK! The shot missed, as at the last instant, aware of the live grenade in his hand, the hero creature took one final step, planted and hurled. Aiming at the crack where the steps were carved, he was deadly accurate. The missile glinted as it plunged deep into the fault—in a second the blast came. But it was muffled, not even an impressive backlash. Nighthawk groaned aloud, lamenting a moment of beauty wasted.

And then the *Yei* proved him wrong. A sound—a gigantic fracturing—wrenched the air as the whole canyon wall tilted outward in slow motion, seemed to hang there an instant before it crashed into the bottoms.

Nighthawk hit the ground, the impact of his body blending with the greater shock. He was blindly aware of bounding boulders, cascades of gravel and boiling dust, he pressed against the earth. He felt her shaking with a great belly laugh, as if she had tired of the antics of her spoilers and decided to play a giant joke on them. Nighthawk laughed with her, his last confusions gone, as the wind scattered the pall of dust.

When he finally got to his feet, shaking off a crust of debris, the Indian sobered quickly. The extent of devastation awed him. The giant sheet of stone had reshaped the whole bottom of the canyon, leaving it clean as if a camp had never existed. Nothing stirred under the impassive sun.

Except the dog. It had outrun the cataclysm and was coming back now, tail at half-mast, needing a friend. Whining, it nosed among the rubble, sniffed at something bright turquoise. The helmet full of stars. It lay a few feet from a huge flake of rock that had wedged against the cliff at an angle, leaving a small space beneath.

Hurrying forward, Nighthawk went down onto his knees, dreading what he might find as he peered into the narrow gap.

From a smudged face, blue eyes blinked at him.

"Scott!" He could hardly hear his own voice through half-deafened ears. "You okay?"

The boy didn't respond. He looked back at the crushed thing, the body of a small lizard, inches from his face. "It's . . . dead," he croaked. And dead is very final, very cold— the shock of a broader comprehension was dawning. In a rush he said, "Gimme a hand, I got to get out of here."

Post-Game Wrap

❑

ACROSS THE majestic bleakness of Dinetah, the two vehicles moved like dedicated ants, one tracking the other. At the wheel of the Bronco, Nighthawk had to ease up on the gas to keep a distance behind the pickup. Jonah wasn't exactly burning up the road. Maybe he needed some time alone with the boy, like she said. Which was the only reason she chose to ride with him in the Bronco—wasn't it? Don't go wishing for miracles.

The Indian told himself, he'd already come out of it with one in his pocket—a whole cave full of thunder and lightning. It was still up there intact, though there was no easy way to reach it now. It would take some fancy chiseling to hack new stairsteps up that raw canyon face. Easier to go down from the rim with ladders, or maybe open a shaft straight through the earth into the cave?

The People could decide that, it was their cave, their munitions dump now.

"You've got to let the Nation have it," he'd told Buford.

[173]

"It's all the chips I've got, if I'm going to get the pols in Washington back to the bargaining table. And it's the only way the tribal council will ever trust me to represent them— if I turn over that fire power."

And Buford had looked totally innocent. "Hey, it's not my ammo. Finders, keepers."

Now all you have to do is deliver that peace pact. A new treaty that will stick, saying the Navajo is to keep his lands forever, to decide where mining can occur and to reap some of the profits. Big job to sell that to Congress. You can't just stand up before their committee and say, "*Ya-tah-hey*, guys, better leave us alone because we're loaded for bear down there. Got a cave full of high-tech death. You try shoving us around, you're history." Nowadays it takes more subtlety to deal with the great white father.

She'd know how, Tall Dove. She'd look at them with those big, sensitive eyes and make them ashamed of their greed, she'd bring out the best in them. I know she does in me.

Are you out of your skull? She probably hopes she never sees you again. This has been an awful hardship on a nice woman, living in a shack, crawling around the rimrock, getting dirty and scratched up. She must be thanking God it's over. Sitting there, staring out at this nowhere country that only a Navajo could appreciate.

And yet she asked if she could keep the badger skin . . .

ISABELL WAS holding it in her lap, her fingers gripping the rich fur as if they were cold. But the truth was, she felt almost too full of body heat, burning with emotions she hardly understood. She only knew she had tasted an excitement that could easily become addictive. Trying to detach herself, she kept her eyes fixed on the distances, but the land just added to her sense of involvement. How she loved it! Such magnificent, primitive beauty . . .

It's not yours, so don't covet it. Or the quiet, courageous man who is so much like it. She tried to force herself back to some frame of mind that would permit her to return to the rut of existence she had left. But a furious insubordination raged through her, lodging in all the secret places of her heart. *I can't. I won't!*

Only what else is there for me? What could I do that would preserve this feeling of incarnation? If there was a faint echo of a snicker far off in the recesses of her memory, she rejected it fiercely. No more ghost powder. No more living a false existence, no more settling for crumbs. Life should be a large piece of cake.

Turning to Nighthawk, whose face reflected the grayness of the November sky, she said, "What does it take to become a paralegal? Good enough to be somebody's assistant in a place like Washington, D.C.?"

And when she saw how the color flooded into his swarthy cheeks, the boyish pleasure that lit his eyes, Isabell knew that for once in her life she had said the right thing.

IN THE truck ahead, Jonah was clenched in silence. Never in his life had he felt so tongue-tied.

Must be the scenery, raw as truth itself. Introspective. Brooding. I can't read it. Can't read the boy— Don't look at him, you'll just get more confused.

Pride doesn't help. It's a terrible constriction, choking off common sense. Making you speechless. Never before lost the ability to communicate. But now, no words. No way to reach out and tell him—God, how I wish—

I must be turning soft.

Well, why not? If I can't have a soft spot for my own son? (Except he's somebody else's now, don't kid yourself.)

But he's my blood. Never quite realized it until back there in the tent—for a handful of minutes we were two of a kind. Doesn't he feel it a little? He called me "Dad." Slip of the tongue. Don't start dreaming a lot of stuff.

And yet I don't sense the hostility anymore. Or the morbidity. Nothing cures your death wishes like a few bullets whittling the rocks around you. Makes you suddenly value every minute—how many men ever learn that?

I could teach him—so much. He's got the makings—the quickness, the smarts, coolness to seize an opportunity. Above all, the luck. He could be better than me . . . Are you out of your mind? You wouldn't wish your kind of life on your worst enemy.

(But I've never been bored, never!)

So—you're a natural. You were born with some weird faculty that goes into "overload" when the chips are down and your life hangs on your next move. It's like a sixth dimension that you learn to live in.

Steve, too, he's got that. "I don't know what makes me jink one way or the other, but I *know*." Telling us about his end-zone run. He must have felt it, at least a little—that high. The pure joy that comes from squeaking your way out of a tight spot. The fiercer the risk, the sweeter the taste of life in your throat afterward. Enjoy it, son!

Or is he sitting there thanking God it's all over? He can get back to his own world, do what? College? Business career? Membership in the country club? Well, why not? A lot of people don't need anymore than that. Anyway, it's none of my affair. Steve, I won't interfere. I'll not bother you again.

I want to be at that graduation in June, but you won't

know I'm there. Rig a disguise. Wouldn't want to put a damper on the celebration. I just need to see you take that big step forward, even if it means you'll walk off into your life with some other guy's hand on your shoulder. Maybe if we'd known each other longer . . .

Forget it! Drive the truck!

SCOTT FELT the slight surge of speed. It gave him a qualm of regret, that this would all be over soon. Even the memory would thin out. Time moves so fast—in a few days Jonah would be half a world away.

That phone call he'd made to his headquarters last night, they'd told him the Shaman had skipped out of South America, heading for India to stir up the Sikhs. India! Make this little side trip seem fairly tame.

Of course there might be a few highlights. Jonah had to remember that scene in the tent. Last night he was like a kid, wanting to hear the rest of the story in detail. Sat there with those beat-up hands draped across the chairback, listening as if he was making a transcript for his personal memory banks. *I think he liked my greasy eggs.*

Just a short nod, but it was better than a medal of honor. Scott was beginning to understand him. There were feelings that couldn't be put into words, especially not by a man who had lived so much alone.

Doesn't he ever wish he had a—maybe not a buddy, but an apprentice? Or does he think I'd flunk the physical? Well, I got news. No more doctors are going to panic me. I ought to know how I feel.

So okay, I accept the fact there'll be no more football, that seemed like an echo out of history anyway. Point is, I am not fragile and the last few days should have proved it. If Jonah doesn't believe me, I've got to make him.

[177]

Because a whole scenario had been building, a future that was looking better by the minute, but he was going to have to sell it carefully, a piece at a time. To his parents, but mostly to Jonah. And right now he needed to take that first step. So keep it offhand, cool.

Out of the silence, in an oddly rusty voice, Scott said, "By the way, just so I'll know— What kind of feathers you plan to wear to my graduation?"

The man beside him glanced across— *Lord! There's the smile I thought he didn't have in him!* Those crazy teeth.

As if invisible windows had been flung open, all at once the old truck seemed full of fresh air. You could breathe. You could think. Like about teeth, for instance. Anyone can afford to lose a few, why not? You could get all kinds of partials—one with a gap-front, make you look like a halfwit. Another with a yellow, crooked grin, turn you utterly evil. Slip 'em on and off . . .

Think about it later. First you have to get your brain pointed back at high school. Buckle down and nail the sheepskin, it always has meant so much to the folks. Mom would cry and Clint would brag to all his friends. Which is why the diploma had to read "Scott Drummond" for old time's sake.

But on my passport—well, the truth is, "Steve Pike" will go better with the trench coat. Right?

ANNABEL and EDGAR JOHNSON live in Denver, Colorado. Before they settled there, however, they traveled the West for years, camping out and collecting background material for their novels. One of their favorite spots is the Navajo Reservation, especially Canyon de Chelly where *Gamebuster* reaches its climax.

Recent young adult novels by the Johnsons include *The Danger Quotient*, *Prisoner of PSI*, and *A Memory of Dragons*. Of the latter, *School Library Journal* said: "The blend of science fiction and political thriller serve as convincing background for this coming-of-age tale."

Their story, *The Grizzly*, won the William Allen White Award. *The Burning Glass* won a Western Writers of America Golden Spur Award.